To my #1 Son with love

Hidden Secret

AUTHOR: C.L. Warner

Cheryl Warner

This book is for my daughter Nanette, with love. Thanks for all your support.

ISBN-13:978-1500212520

AFTER 2 YEARS OF MARRAGE, BRIAN HIRES HIS FRIEND, JASON STONE, TO WORK FOR HIM ON HIS RANCH. WHILE BRIAN IS WORKING HARD TO CATCH A SERIAL KILLER, JASON IS FALLING IN LOVE WITH BRIAN'S WIFE, BRENDA.
AS THE KILLER SETS HIS SIGHTS ON BRENDA, JASON BECOMES ONE OF BRIAN'S SUSPECTS WHEN INCRIMINATING EVIDENCE IS FOUND IN HIS HOME.

HIDDEN SECRET IS PART 2, OF BRENDA HOLLISTER'S STORY.
READ PART 1 IN, **THE SECRET OF SILVER LAKE PASS**

All names and places depicted in this book are fictional and
used for entertainment purposes only:

CHAPTER 1

Brenda stood at the kitchen window looking out at the dark fast moving clouds as they rolled across the sky. Winter was on its way and there was still a lot of work to be done around the ranch before the cold weather set in. September 25th thought Brenda. Had it really been two years since she and Brian had said, "I do?" She could still recall that day as if it were yesterday. She was standing at the back of a quaint little church, waiting to walk down the aisle dressed in her beautiful wedding gown.

She remembered being excited at the thought of becoming Mrs. Brian Nichols, but her nerves remained calm. She knew she loved Brian and he loved her, so she couldn't understand why she became so anxious when the wedding march began to play.

She smiled as she remembered walking down the aisle with her father and seeing Brian's face light up when he saw her in her dress. Both Brian and Allen had both looked very handsome standing there in their tucks. Who would have ever thought that Brian and Allen would become good friends and Brian would ask him to be his best man, especially when both men had competed for her affection. Yes, they made quite a pair, those two, thought Brenda.

Brenda couldn't forget Allen telling Brian at their reception that he still felt he would have been a better choice for Brenda, and if Brian didn't take good care of her, he would come back and steal her away. Brian told him he could try, but he better be a fast runner, because he wouldn't hesitate to shoot him in the ass if he tried.

The timer went off, bringing Brenda back to the present.

As she lifted a rib roast from the oven, she heard the phone ring. It was Brian, calling to say he'd be working late again tonight.

There had been another murder. Only this time the body was found just outside their little town of Cambridge and because Brian was assigned as lead Detective, he would have to stay late and run down leads.

Brian sat at his desk looking through the case folder as he spoke to Brenda. It held pictures of several young women whose bodies were found over the past few months and now he had to add another one to the folder.

"It looks like our serial killer is at it again," he told Brenda.

"That's so scary," said Brenda. "Do you still think he's someone who lives in the area?"

Brenda could hear the concern in Brian's voice when he replied. "It's possible. So far all of the victim's bodies have been found within a fifty mile radius of here and all the women have worked in or around Cambridge."

"Babe, I'm sorry but I have to go. I just wanted to let you know I wouldn't be home until late and not to wait up for me."

Brenda felt disappointed as she looked at the dinner she had just prepared, the anniversary gift and cake she had sitting on the table.

"But I just fixed us a nice dinner."

"I'm sorry babe. You know I'd much rather be there with you, then stuck here running down leads."

"I know," Brenda said. She thought about all the time she had spent fixing a special dinner and now it was for nothing.

"Well don't worry about things here. I've already fed the horses and bedded them down for the night, but it still sucks that I have to spend our anniversary alone."

"Thanks honey."

Brian paused. Had he heard her right? Did she just say it was their anniversary?

Brian quickly looked at the calendar on his desk. Oh, crap!

"Honey I'm so sorry! I've been so tied up with this case I forgot what day it was."

"Well I just want you to know I baked a cake and made all your favorite foods!"

Great, now I really feel like a jerk, thought Brian.

"I promise, I'll make it up to you."

"I know you will! So don't come home tired and complaining about having a headache!" teased Brenda.

"Don't worry, I can promise you that won't happen!"

"I love you honey."

"I love you too babe and I'm really sorry I can't be there with you."

"I know. Goodnight darling."

"Goodnight honey. Try to have a good night and make sure you lock all the doors before you go to bed."

"I will. Love you."

"Love you too."

Brenda had a feeling that Brian would be working late more often now that this case had been assigned to him, but it still didn't make her feel any better as she sat down and stared at her roast.

The following day, Brenda had barely arrived home from work when she heard a car pull in.

She wasn't expecting Brian, so she looked out her bedroom window to see who had pulled in.

To her surprise and excitement, it was Brian. Hurrying to the kitchen door, she greeted him with a kiss as he walked in.

"I can't believe it! You're actually home early for a change?" she said cheerfully.

"I knew you'd be surprised," he said, as he gave Brenda a long lingering kiss.

"Sorry about last night. I felt really bad about ruining your dinner and not being here to celebrate our anniversary."

"Well you're here now and that's all that matters," said Brenda, giving Brian another kiss.

Brian was holding a big bouquet of flowers and a small, neatly wrapped gift, which he now handed to her.

"These are for you honey. Happy anniversary."

Brenda looked at Brian and smiled.

"Thank you darling. These flowers are beautiful." Brenda arranged the flowers in a vase and sat them on the table. "Thanks honey, they're beautiful."

"You're welcome. Now open this," Brian said, full of anticipation.

"Oh Brian, their gorgeous!" said Brenda, as she stared at the Marquise cut diamond earrings.

"Now if you don't like them, you can take them back and pick something else out."

"Are you kidding? I love them. They're perfect darling, thank you."

"Wait here," said Brenda, as she hurried to the bedroom.

When she came back, she had a gift in her hand and handed it to Brian.

"Happy anniversary darling. I hope you like it."

"I'm sure I will. I haven't gotten anything from you yet that I haven't liked."

Brian opened the box and inside he found the watch he had been admiring for some time now.

Smiling, he slid his arms around Brenda's waist and said, "How did you know I wanted this watch?"

"I keep an eye on you when we go shopping and I can tell when you really like something."

"Thanks honey. It's perfect."

Brian gave Brenda a kiss and then Brenda said, "Why don't you get cleaned up while I warm up the food I fixed for dinner last night?"

"Good idea. I'm starved."

When Brian came out of the bathroom, Brenda asked, "So what's been happening with the case?"

"Not much I'm afraid. Every time we think we have a solid lead, it turns out to be another dead end."

"Do I have time to go to the barn and take care of the horses before we eat?"

"Can't we do that after we eat? You have to be exhausted and the chores can wait a little longer."

"I'd rather do it now before I get comfortable. It

won't take me long. Besides I haven't been to the barn in so long I'm afraid Charger won't remember me."

"That is a possibility," said Brenda, as she looked over her shoulder at Brian and smiled.

"I know I had a hard time recognizing you."

"You are the mailman aren't you?" she teased.

"No, I'm the cop who's going to handcuff you and put you under house arrest right after I strip search you!" Brian grabbed Brenda by the butt cheeks, pulled her up against him, and began kissing her neck.

Goose bumps raced up and down Brenda's arms as Brian's warm breath and kisses caressed her throat.

"Stop that, you're giving me goose bumps," she laughed, as she smacked him on the butt and tried to push him away.

"Go do your chores!"

As Brian walked back to the house, he was aware that the weather was changing fast, and that he was going to have to hire someone to help him bring the cattle up from the summer pasture and get their shelters ready for winter. He looked over at the pile of wood that still needed to be split and stacked. The work seemed to be piling up and he didn't like the fact that he had to be away from the ranch when there was so much that needed to be done. He missed being home at night, and the fact that he and Brenda hadn't been able to spend much time together lately, was also bothering him.

As they sat down for dinner, Brenda decided to ask what she could do to help around the ranch.

"I know you said you didn't want me messing with the wood splitter, but if you'll show me how to operate the thing, I could probably get most of that wood split and stacked, which would be one less chore we have to worry about," said Brenda.

"Honey, you already have your hands full with working full time at Regions and taking care of the house. Not to mention you're taking care of the horses every night!" said Brian.

"Besides I wouldn't be comfortable having you run the splitter when no one's around to keep an eye on you."

"But you already told me you didn't have any idea how much longer this case will take and we're starting to run out of time!"

"What if I cut my hours at Regions down to part time? Then I'd have the time to help out more."

"I still wouldn't want you using the splitter! It's too dangerous and besides that's not a job for a woman."

"Look, you know I'd love to have you go to part time. I wouldn't care if you quit your job altogether, if that's what you wanted. But I don't want you doing it because you feel you have to in order to help out around here!"

Brenda sat there quietly as she considered the idea of going to part time. She enjoyed her job at Regions, but she loved working around home even more. She knew Brian wouldn't mind if she quit altogether because he wanted to start a family, but she wasn't sure she was ready for children.

Brian interrupted Brenda's thoughts when he said, "I've been considering hiring someone to help out around here for a while. We could use an extra hand around here and I'd feel better having someone around I could trust to look after things when I'm not here."

"What do you think?"

"I didn't realize you were thinking about hiring someone, but to be honest, I think it's a great idea."

"Did you have anyone in mind?"

"There are a couple of guys I'm considering. I just haven't had a chance to talk to them about it yet. I'll try and get a hold of them sometime tomorrow to see if they're interested."

"Sounds good to me," said Brenda, as she got up and started clearing the table. "I'll leave that up to you to figure out, but I still might cut my hours to part time."

"Well you know whatever you decide will be fine with me."

Brenda was busy in the kitchen cleaning up. She was trying to hurry because she could hear Brian in the den, building a fire in the fireplace. It seemed like it had been a lot longer to Brenda, than a couple of weeks since she and Brian had spent any quality time together and she couldn't wait to snuggle up with him in front of the fireplace. When she had finally finished, she walked into the den and sat down on the couch. Brian had been stoking the fire but stopped when Brenda entered the room. Walking over to the couch, he picked up the pillows that Brenda had neatly placed across the back and began tossing them onto the floor.

"Why don't you come down here and join me?" he said, as he lay down on the floor and propped his head up on the pillows.

Brenda smiled as she got up and lay down next to him. The fire warmed their bodies and the glow from the fireplace made the whole room feel cozy and romantic. Brian put his arm around Brenda and kissed her full soft lips tenderly. Rolling onto her side, she slid her leg over his and rested her head on his shoulder.

"You look tired," she said, with concern in her voice as she studied Brian's face.

"I'm not that tired," he said, as he slipped his hand under her sweater and began fondling her round firm breasts.

"What are you up to Detective?" she teased.

"I was thinking about stripping off all your clothes and making wild passionate love to you," said Brian, as he pulled her on top of him and pulled her sweater off over her head.

"Really? I think I might enjoy that!" said Brenda with a sly little grin.

It had been a long time since they had made love to each other, so as their kisses grew more and more passionate and their fondling became more intimate, a hunger and fire ignited between them that they hadn't felt for some time. Brian quickly began pulling at the rest of Brenda's clothes, marveling at her shapely naked body.

Brenda unzipped Brian's pants and pulled his shirt open, exposing his muscular chest.

Brian got up quickly and removed the rest of his clothing before lying back down next to his wife. Her naked body felt warm and soft next to his as he slid his arms around her and pulled her close to him.

Brenda went to roll on top of Brian, but found her long hair was pinned under his shoulder.

"Brian, you're on my hair."

"Sorry," he said, quickly leaned forward and hitting Brenda in the forehead with his head.

"Ouch! You don't have to knock me out! I'm a sure thing, remember?" giggled Brenda.

"I'm really sorry," chuckled Brian.

"I always knew you had a hard head," said Brenda, as she rubbed her forehead.

"Here, let me kiss it," he said, pulling her to him and gently kissing her forehead.

Brenda gazed into Brian's eyes and then captured his mouth with hers. Slipping her tongue into his mouth with all the sensuality of a temptress, she teased and tasted him.

She slid her hands down the length of his body, kissing his chest while she slowly continued her downward descent to his stomach. Reaching between her legs, she took a hold of his penis and began massaging its head between the lips of her vagina. She could hear Brian's breathing become heavy and more and more ragged as she continued to stimulate him. His penis had swollen hard in her hand, so she slowly lowered herself onto him. Brian moaned as he felt his manhood go deep inside her. Feeling the warmth and wet sweetness of her vagina aroused him even more as he placed his hands onto her hips and pulled her down onto him.

She slowly began moving her body up and down the length of his shaft and then in circles as she moaned and kissed his lips hungrily.

Brian was desperately fighting his urge to come inside her, but he she wasn't ready yet.

As Brenda's need for him grew more urgent, she began moving her body up and down, faster and faster, causing her to cry out as her own aroused body yearned to climax.

Brian knew he couldn't hold out much longer as he rolled on top on her. Losing his penetration, he quickly thrust his body against hers, driving his swollen penis deep inside her. Each kiss grew deeper than the next as they moved in time with each other's body. The urgency of their lovemaking made their passion for each other soar higher than ever before. Brian felt the muscles in Brenda's legs tighten as she moaned and arched her body against his. "Harder," she begged.

"Yes, yes, right there. Oh god, that feels so good." Her voice was raspy and full of lust as Brian moved his body against hers at a fevered pace. He was ready to come at any moment when he heard Brenda cry out in a husky voice, "Oh God! I'm going to come!"

Brian felt Brenda's body strain against his. She pressed her head against the pillows and dug her fingers into his hips. "Oh Brian," she cried.

"Oh God...Oh God don't stop!"

Brian felt her shiver as she climaxed and then a moment later, she relaxed. All her pent up desires had been released from her warm, sultry body.

Brian moaned as he thrust his body against hers one last time before erupting inside her.

They lay quietly in front of the fire totally spent as

they continued to cling to each other.

Still relishing the feelings of their lovemaking, Brenda sighed and said, "We really need to do this more often."

"We will, I promise," said Brian, feeling guilty for working so many late hours.

"I'm sorry that I've been neglecting you lately."

"I know that it can't be helped," said Brenda, turning and giving him a kiss.

"I just hope you catch that guy. And soon!"

The following day Brenda was at work having lunch when she received a phone call from Brian.

"I think I have our problem solved," said Brian.

"I thought we solved our problem last night," teased Brenda.

"I wasn't talking about that problem. I was talking about getting some help at the ranch! I got a call this morning from one of my friends who used to play polo. It seems the place where he works, cut back on his hours, so he had to move and now he's looking for a place to board his horse and is looking to pick up some extra work."

"That sounds great!" said Brenda.

"I kind of figured you'd feel that way, so I went ahead and hired him. He'll probably be at the house when you get home tonight."

"Oh, ok," said Brenda.

"I think I should let you know that I did decide to

cut my hours to part time."

"That's great, but are you sure that's what you really want to do?"

"I'm sure. You don't mind do you?"

"No, why would I? I kind of like the idea of you being home more."

"So is this friend of yours bringing his horse out tonight?"

"I think so. His name's Jason Stone. I told him he could put his horse in the empty stall next to Charger's and that you should be home shortly after he gets there."

"Ok, good," said Brenda.

"Jason's a good guy and I've heard he's a hard worker. I think you'll like him."

"I'm sure I will," said Brenda. "I'm just glad you found someone."

"Will you be home for dinner tonight?"

"I'm not sure, but I'll try. If I'm not there before Jason's ready to leave, tell him I'll give him a call later on tonight and fill him in on what needs to be done."

"Ok, I'll tell him," said Brenda.

"I've got to go babe, but I'll try to make it home in time for dinner."

"Alright, but I'm not going to hold my breath."

"Talk to you later. Love you," said Brenda.

"Love you too."

When Brenda pulled up to the house, she noticed a black truck with a horse trailer attached to it, backed up to the barn. The barn doors were open and the lights were on, but she didn't see anyone around. She pulled into the garage and went inside to change her clothes before heading down to the barn to introduce herself to Jason.

When Brenda walked into the barn, she still couldn't find Jason, but she did notice a beautiful bay mare standing in the stall next to Charger's stall.

As Brenda looked around, she noticed that both Hank and Charger's stalls had already been cleaned and fresh bedding had been put down for them. Feed and fresh water had also been put in each of their stalls, leaving Brenda to believe that Brian had done the right thing by hiring Jason.

Brenda walked out of the barn by way of the back door and noticed a man walking across the pasture toward the horses. Brenda's horse Hank, was also watching the man. As Jason got closer, Hank stomped his foot, laid his ears back and tossed his head to warn him not to come any closer. Brenda knew Hank wasn't fond of men, so she whistled loudly to get her horses attention. Jason turned and looked in Brenda's direction as Hank charged past him, shaking his head and kicking to show his dislike of strangers. Jason jumped out of the way, as both horses galloped past him toward the gate.

Brenda was waiting with a peppermint candy for each of them as they walked up to her. She rubbed their heads and told them what good boys they were as she snapped a lead to each of their halters and waited for Jason.

When Jason reached the gate, he said, "Hi, you must be Brenda. I'm Jason Stone."

"It's nice to meet you Jason. Brian said you would probably be here when I got home. I see you've already been hard at work."

"Well I figured since I was bedding down my horse, I might as well do the other two stalls."

Brenda opened the gate and led the horses through.

"Well this bad tempered boy is Hank," she said, patting her horse's neck. "And I'm assuming you already know Charger, since Brian tells me the two of you played polo together."

"Yeah, I remember Charger," replied Jason, as he patted Charger on the back. "Hey old man, it's been a long time hasn't it?"

As they headed for the barn, Brenda said, "Did Brian tell you he took me to my first polo match on our first date, and if I remember correctly I think you were playing that day."

"That's possible," said Jason.

"When I walked into the barn and saw your mare, she looked familiar and I rarely forget a horse. Then

I remembered she was one of the horses that caught my eye at the polo match. She was really fast and agile and I also remember you were one of the team's better players."

"Thanks, I try."

"So tell me, did we win that day?"

"No, I'm afraid not," chuckled Brenda.

Brenda couldn't help but notice what a nice smile Jason had when he said, "That doesn't surprise me."

"I'm afraid our team has never been the same since Brian left."

"That's what I've been told. I'm sorry I never got to see him play."

"You would have been impressed. He and old Charger were quite the pair."

Jason liked Brenda right away. She was easy to talk to and she made him feel right at home.

Brenda put the horses in their stalls and as she closed Hank's stall door she said, "I think you better let me take Hank in and out of the barn. Nothing against you! He's just not too fond of men. He still gives Brian trouble sometimes, and he knows him."

"Ok," said Jason thoughtfully. "I'll just wait to clean his stall after you turn him out."

"That'd be great," said Brenda.

"We're not sure what happened to him before Dr. Patel got him, but Dr. Patel did say he was rescued from a man who beat and starved him. I don't think he would have gotten him if it hadn't been for his wife. She felt sorry for him and insisted that her husband adopt him."

"Well I usually get along pretty well with horses, so maybe in time he'll come around," said Jason, as he walked over to Hank's stall door and looked in. Hank quickly flattened his ears and charged the stall door, causing Jason to jump back. "Or maybe not!"

"Stop that Hank!" scolded Brenda, as she pushed him away from the door.

"I'm sorry," apologized Brenda. "Like I said, he doesn't care for men."

"Well I don't think I'll be foolish enough to go walking into the pasture with him again," chuckled Jason.

"Yeah, I don't think that would be very wise. "

"I'm surprised Brian didn't warn you about him."

"Nope, he never said a word. Maybe he was afraid I wouldn't take the job."

"Maybe," chuckled Brenda.

"Well if you want, you can turn your horse out in the pasture with Charger and I'll put Hank in the smaller pasture next to them."

"Alright, that works for me."

"Oh, before I forget, Brian said he'd give you a call later tonight and explain what needs to be done around here."

"Ok, thanks."

"Well, I better get back to the house and start dinner."

"It's going to be nice to have some extra help around here," said Brenda as she walked out of the barn.

"Will you be here around the same time tomorrow?" asked Jason.

"I should be," said Brenda. "Have a good night."

"You too, and it was nice meeting you Brenda."

Jason watched as Brenda left the barn and made her way back to the house.

Brenda opened the door and was about to walk inside when Brian came pulling in. Astonished that he had made it home so early, she raced over to his car and threw her arms around his neck. Brian smiled and lifted her off the ground, giving her a big hug and a kiss.

"This is a pleasant surprise," she said as he sat her back down. "I didn't expect you home this early."

"Well as it turned out, I didn't need to stay late tonight."

"Have you had a chance to meet Jason yet?"

"Yes and he seems very nice."

"Yeah, he's a good guy."

"Hank didn't think much of him though."

"Hank doesn't think much of any men! He didn't scare him off did he?"

"No, but he's working on it."

"I'm going to head down to the barn and see how

he's doing. I'll be up in a few minutes."

"Ok, take your time. I was just going in to start dinner."

Brenda was heading to the house when Brian called out to her. "Brenda! Would you mind if I ask Jason to stay and eat with us tonight?"

"No, not at all," she replied.

As Brian and Jason made their way to the house, Brian's co-worker, Detective Steven Wade, came pulling in. He rolled down his window and called out to Brian.

"Brian! Another body was just found about ten miles from here on old Stony Road."

Brian walked over to Steve and after a short conversation, Jason heard Brian telling Steve he'd be right behind him.

Brian found it odd that the station hadn't called him about the body, but Steve explained that he was close by when he got the call and said he would stop and get Brian on his way.

"Sorry man, but I have to go," Brian told Jason.

"I'll get going too then," Jason told Brian, knowing that Brian would be leaving before they had a chance to eat.

Brenda came out of the house to see what was going on and Brian told her that Steve stopped to let him know another body had been discovered and he had to go.

"Alright," said a disappointed Brenda.

"I'm sorry about dinner honey. I'll give you a call later."

"Ok," said Brenda.

"Jason, you'll stay and eat won't you?"

"I think it would be best if I go too."

"Well at least let me send some of this food home with you."

Jason looked at Brian and Brian said, "You better do what she says."

Then Brian kissed Brenda goodbye and headed for his car.

Brenda invited Jason into the house while she packaged up his food.

"This is really a nice place you have here," said Jason.

"Thank you. We really like it," said Brenda.

"I used to come out here and ride when Dr. Patel owned it, but I never dreamed I'd be living here."

"I remember Brian telling me he'd like to buy this place," said Jason.

"Here you go," said Brenda, as she handed Jason a plastic container filled with food.

"Thanks, I really appreciate this, but I'm sorry you went to all this trouble for nothing."

"Don't be sorry. I'm used to it," Brenda said with a smile.

"Well, I better get going. Thanks again for the food."

"I'll bring your dish back to you tomorrow."

"No hurry. Have a good night Jason."

"You too."

Jason left, leaving Brenda to eat another dinner alone.

As Brian walked toward the crime scene, one of the officers said, "Her body's right over here Detective."

Brian could see a young woman's naked body lying face down in the field.

"What have you got for me Ed?" Brian asked the medical examiner.

"Same as the others," he replied. "The victim's a woman in her twenties. Her hands and feet are bound with duct tape and she was shot in the head with a 38 caliber hand gun."

"A 38? All the other women were shot with a 40 caliber."

"Do you think it's a copy cat murder?"

"I don't know, but from the bruises on her arms and legs I'd say she put up quite a fight."

Brian couldn't help but feel frustration and anger as he stood looking at the young woman's lifeless body. None of these senseless murders made any sense to him and he wanted desperately to find the person responsible for this before he has a chance to kill again.

Brian looked around the crime scene for any

evidence that may have been left behind by the killer. When he came up empty handed, he tried to retrace the path the killer may have taken from the road to where he had dumped the body.

He knew how careful the killer had been not to leave any evidence, but as Brian walked up the embankment to the road, he spotted a cigarette butt and some tire tracks. Slipping on a glove, he bent down and picked the cigarette up. As he dropped it into a bag, he hoped that cigarette butt would be their first real clue to finding their murderer.

Brian sat at his desk looking again at the pictures of the young women who had fallen victim to the killer. He knew the chance of that cigarette butt belonging to him was slim, but he still couldn't help but hope that something would come of it.

Down in the lab, the forensic pathologist was finishing her examination of the latest victim's body. She picked up her phone and dialed Brian's number. "Detective, I think you should come to the lab. I may have something for you."

When Brian walked into the lab, he noticed the young woman's body lying on a table, with the examiner standing over her.

"I hope you have some good news for me," Brian said.

"Well I do have a couple of things that I think you might find interesting."

"This victim died from a 38 caliber gunshot wound to the head, unlike the other women who were all killed with a 40 caliber. The other thing that makes this murder different from the others is that the women killed with the 40 caliber were shot at point blank range. Whereas this woman was shot at close range."

" Which means what?" asked Brian.

"It means the person who shot this girl was standing about three feet away from her when he pulled the trigger."

"Also this girl was sexually molested, and from the bruising on her arms and legs, I'd say she must have put up quite a fight. I also recovered some tissue from under her fingernails and some semen."

"What do you know, our killer finally screwed up," Brian said thoughtfully.

"He tried to clean her up after he killed her, but fortunately for us, he didn't do a very good job."

Brian felt nothing but disgust for this killer and hoped the DNA would come up with a match.

"Anything else?"

"Just this."

The pathologist showed Brian a burn mark on the young woman's neck.

"Is that what I think it is?"

"It's a cigarette burn."

Brian's heart began to pound as he thought about that cigarette butt he found lying beside the road. "She was already dead when she was burned, so my guess is, he had a cigarette in his mouth when he lifted her body out of his car and accidently burned her neck with it."

Brian could finally see a glimmer of hope as he returned to his office. Now all they had to do was wait for the DNA results to come back from the Lab and hope for a match.

That evening Brian held a briefing with the other investigating officers who were working the case. When the briefing concluded, Brian told Steve he was going to call it a night and head home.

"Why don't we celebrate and go out for a beer?" Steve asked Brian.

"I can't. I have to get home."

Disappointed Steve shook his head in dismay and said, "You're just like all the other guys. Why is it all you married men have to rush home to your old ladies and what was Jason doing at your place?" asked Steve.

"He's going to be helping me out at the ranch for awhile."

Steve was taken back for a moment and then asked, "Do you think that's wise?"

"What are you getting at Steve?"

"I just thought you would have wised up after that Allen guy and you know how women act when they get around Jason," suggested Steve.

"What are you talking about?"

"They go all goo-goo over his big muscles and rugged looks. I swear, that guy has a new woman every other week," Steve said sarcastically.

"Well even if that were true, how is that my problem?" asked Brian.

"I'm just saying you better keep an eye on him around your wife. If he's going to be spending a lot of time at the ranch alone with Brenda...well you just never know."

"Thanks for the advice, but I trust my wife and I have no reason not to trust Jason."

"Ok, but don't say I didn't warn you."

"Ok Steve, I'll be sure to keep that in mind, since I don't have anything better to worry about!"

Brian straightened up his desk and headed for the door with Steve following close behind him.

Still trying to drive his point home, Steve said, "I can't believe you'd want Jason hanging when you know he's been in trouble before."

"What the hell is your problem with Jason all of a sudden?" asked Brian

"Nothing, but he does have a record. Or have you forgotten that?" Steve replied.

"No, I haven't forgotten! But that was a long time ago and he was a kid when that happened!"
"He paid his dues and he's been clean since then, so just drop it!" said Brian.
"Whatever," said Steve.

 When Brian pulled up to the house, he was still irritated with Steve. He wished Steve would learn to keep his mouth shut and mind his own business. Brian knew Steve had a chip on his shoulder for asking Allen to be his best man at his wedding instead of him, but he never intended to ask Steve anyway. He knew Steve never cared for Brenda and was against the marriage. But it had been two years since the wedding and if that was what was still bothering him, he better get over it before he ruined what little bit of friendship they have left.

As Steve opened his car door, he was thinking, "Maybe Brian thinks he can trust that wife of his around Jason, but I'm not as blind as he is. Just because he trusts her, doesn't mean I do!"
 Steve had never forgotten how Brian had risked his life for him when he was a rookie but he also hadn't forgotten about the wedding and he blamed Brenda for that.
Steve remembered that up until Brian met Brenda, he had been Brian's best friend and the person Brian

hung out with on the weekends and after work. But Steve felt Brenda had changed all that by turning Brian against him, and Steve resented her for it.

So he made himself a promise that night.

He would expose Brenda for what she really was.

A smart mouthed lying little cheat.

CHAPTER 2

It was a beautiful fall Saturday and Brenda was having coffee with Brian when they noticed Jason pull in and head for the barn.

"He's here bright and early," said Brenda.

"Well I told him I wanted to go down to the back pasture today and bring the cattle up to the winter pasture. I didn't think he'd come quite this early though."

"I guess I better get around and go down there."

When Brian came out of the bedroom, he pulled on his jacket and Brenda handed him two cups of coffee.

"Here's some coffee for you and Jason."

"Thanks babe. Aren't you going with us?"

"I'll be down in a few minutes. Don't leave without me!" she told Brian as he walked out the door.

"I wouldn't dream of it," he said in a teasing voice.

"Morning Jason," said Brian, as he walked into the barn.

Jason was already busy feeding the horses and had not heard Brian come in. He jumped when he turned around and saw Brian standing behind him.

"Hey Brian."

"A little jumpy aren't you?" teased Brian.

"I didn't hear you come in."

"Brenda thought you might like some coffee."

"Thanks," said Jason, taking the cup from Brian and warming his hands with it.

"Are you still planning on bringing the cattle up to the winter pasture today?"

"Yeah, we'll round them up and drive them down the lane to the smaller pasture where the shelters are. Then we'll need to check the water lines out there to make sure they're all wrapped with insulation."

"What are you doing about the corn field? That corn's ready to be harvested too."

"I rent that field to the neighbor down the road, so that's his worry."

Brenda walked into the barn a few moments later and noticed the guys sitting around talking. After saying "Hello" to Jason, she entered Hank's stall. She noticed that Jason had already fed him, so she picked up a brush and began brushing him.

When she had finished, she sat down on a bale of straw and listened as Brian and Jason reminisced about their polo days.

After about twenty minutes, Brenda was becoming impatient and wanted to get going.

"Are you two going to sit here all day talking, or are we going to get something done?"

Both men looked at each other in surprise and then quickly got to their feet. A smile crossed Brian's face.

"I guess we better get a move on before my wife gets the bullwhip out."

Brian and Jason smiled as Brenda headed for the tack room with the walk of a determined foreman.

The three of them saddled up and rode down the lane to where the cattle were spread out over a large span of pasture. Brian opened the gate and they rode through and fanned out. As they herded the cattle into one tight group, Brenda couldn't help but notice how skillfully the two men worked together. She was thankful Hank knew what to do, because she still hadn't mastered the herding techniques of the men.

As they drove the cattle down the lane toward the winter pasture, Brenda heard Brian's cell phone ring. She knew something was up by the look on his face as he spoke to the person on the other end of the line. Oh please, don't let there be another body, Brenda thought to herself.

After they had all of the cattle into their new pasture, Brian closed the gate behind them and rode over to Jason and Brenda.

All he said was, "I have to go into the station."

"Ok," said Jason. "Don't worry about the water lines.

I'll make sure they're all wrapped."

"Thanks man."

Brian leaned into Brenda and gave her a kiss.

"Sorry babe. I'll call you later," he said and then he headed for the barn at a full gallop.

"He's got a tough job," said Jason.

"I know," sighed Brenda. "This case is really starting to get to him."

They road back to the barn and after putting the horses away, Brenda said, "I'm going in, but if you need anything just let me know."

"Thanks, but I think I'm good," replied Jason.

By lunchtime, Brenda still hadn't heard from Brian so she headed over to the winter pasture where she found Jason hard at work wrapping water lines.

"Jason, why don't you take a break and come up to the house with me. I made some sandwiches and a pot of hot coffee to warm you up while we eat.

"I don't want to intrude," Jason replied, uncertain as to whether or not he should go inside without Brian being there.

"You're not intruding and besides I'm getting tired of eating alone."

"I don't know. I really think I should get this done."

"Those pipes have waited this long, so I'm sure they can wait long enough for you to get something to eat! And if you're worried about how Brian, don't

be! He wouldn't want me to let his right hand man
starve to death."
"Ok, if you're sure it's no problem."
 "Trust me, its fine."
As they walked back to the house together, a strange
feeling came over Brenda. She felt as if someone
was watching them. She looked around, but when
she didn't see anyone, she quickly shrugged it off.

Brian glanced at the clock and picked up the phone
to call Brenda. He finally had some good news to tell
her about the case.
"Hi Babe," said Brian. "I'm sorry I ran out on you
and Jason this morning."
"That's alright. So what's going on?"
"The DNA report came back and it matched a guy
named Calvin Knight. It seems he was released from
prison about six months ago, which is about the
same time the murders started. We're trying to
locate him now."
"Well I hope you can find him before he kills anyone
else!"
"How are things there?" asked Brian.
"Fine. Jason's been working on the water lines and
now we're eating some lunch."
"Do you have any idea when you'll be home?"
"It's really hard to say. I'll have to call you later
when I have a better idea."

"Hey Babe, put Jason on the phone for a minute, will you?"

"Sure, hold on."

"Hey Brian what's up?" said Jason.

"Hey Jason. I was wondering how long you were planning on staying today."

"I'm not sure. Do you have something else you want me to do before I go?"

"No, but I need to know if you'll do me a favor."

"Sure."

"I'd really appreciate it if you could hang around long enough to feed the horses tonight. We think the serial killer could be hiding out in one of the hunting lodges in the woods, across the road. I'd rather Brenda not go to the barn by herself until we catch this guy."

"Sure, I can stay and do that for you," said Jason, trying not to alert Brenda to Brian's concerns.

"Thanks man, I really appreciate it."

"No problem."

Jason and Brian said goodbye and then Jason handed the phone back to Brenda. She continued to talk to Brian for a few more minutes before hanging up.

When Jason had finished his lunch, he thanked Brenda for the coffee and sandwich's and excused himself. As he headed back to the winter pasture, he had the same strange feeling that Brenda had had earlier, that someone was watching him. He looked around but after not seeing any sign of anyone, he went back to work.

Around five o'clock Benda was surprised to find that Jason's truck was still parked out by the barn. She decided she better go down and check to make sure nothing had happened to him since she hadn't seen him since lunch.

"You're staying awfully late for a Saturday night!" said Brenda as she entered the barn and found Jason brushing his horse.
 "No hot date tonight?" she teased.
"Not tonight," smiled Jason. "I thought I might as well stick around and take care of the horses before I leave."
"That's really nice of you, but I really don't mind doing the chores and I think you've already done more than your share of work around here today."
"It's really no trouble and I enjoy being out here with the horses."
"I know what you mean. I'd rather be in the barn doing chores, then cooped up in the house cleaning."
Jason and Brenda both heard a car coming down the driveway and went to see who it was. Brenda walked out of the barn with Jason close behind her. Jason was relieved when he saw Brian, pull up to the garage and climb out of his car. He was quickly

running out of excuses for why he was hanging around so long.

Brian noticed the two of them standing in the barn doorway and walked down to join them.

"Did you have any luck finding him?" Brenda asked Brian anxiously.

"Not yet," said Brian.

"We have his place staked out, but it doesn't look like he's been there for awhile."

"He always seems to be one step ahead of us, but at least we're getting closer. Hopefully it won't be too much longer."

"Have you eaten yet?"

"Yeah, I grabbed a couple of burgers in town."

"Well, I'm out of here," said Jason. "I'll see you two Monday morning."

"Ok," said Brian, "and thanks."

"No problem."

Steve was pacing around his apartment seething with anger.

"I knew it! Once a cheat always a cheat!" he told himself.

"Well I have to give it to you Brenda, you sure didn't waste any time did you? Well you're not going to get away with it this time you little tramp, because I plan on exposing you and your new boyfriend!

Brian may be blind when it comes to you two, but you can't fool me! We'll see how much he trusts you when I get done with you!"

 It was a chilly Sunday morning and Brenda had gotten up early to fix breakfast.
Brian came walking into the kitchen and Brenda said, "Good morning sleepy head."
"Good morning. Something sure smells good," said Brian, as he poured himself a cup of coffee.
"I'm making French toast and bacon."
"So what's on your schedule for today?" asked Brenda.
"I thought I'd get started on that wood pile."
"I can help you with that," said Brenda, as she sat Brian's breakfast down in front of him.
"Are you sure? It's pretty nippy out there this morning and I know today's the day you usually do your shopping."
"I'm sure. I'd rather spend time with you, besides I can go shopping anytime."
Brian gave Brenda a kiss, "And that's why I love you," he said.

Brenda was finishing up in the kitchen while Brian was getting the wood splitter ready. When she glanced out the window to see if Brian was ready to start, she noticed Jason's truck coming down the driveway. She was surprised and a little disappointed when she saw him pull in. She had been looking forward to spending the whole day alone with her husband.

She watched from the kitchen window as Brian and Jason talked. Slipped on her coat, she walked out onto the porch and noticed Jason heading for the barn. She walked over to Brian.

"Did you ask Jason to come out today to help with the wood?" asked Brenda.

"No," replied Brian. "He's here to work his horse." Brenda watched as Jason led Star from the barn to the round pen and turned her loose.

As Brenda stacked the wood, she continued to keep an eye on Jason and Star. Finally, she paused so she could watch more closely. She had never seen anyone work a horse the way Jason was working Star. Brenda soon became mesmerized as she watched them. It didn't take long before Brian realized that Brenda had stopped working to watch Jason. The wood he had been splitting was quickly piling up around his feet.

Turning off the splitter, Brian said, "He really has a way with horses doesn't he?"

"I guess so! I've never seen anything like it!"

"It's as if his horse is reading his mind."

"I know. That's why the guys on the polo team

called him the horse whisperer."

"Well I can understand why they would!" said Brenda as she watched in amazement.

"So are you going to finish helping me, or would you rather watch Jason?" teased Brian.

Brenda looked at the pile of wood next to Brian's feet, "Sorry," she said.

"I'll get back to work."

Brian and Brenda were close to being finished when Brian's phone rang.

"Damn it Steve! How did that happen?"

Brenda could hear the frustration in Brian's voice as he talked to Steve. When he hung up, he looked at Brenda with a disgusted look on his face.

"What now," asked Brenda?

"The guy we've been hunting for... he was stopped in Montgomery for a traffic violation and they let him go!"

"You've got to be kidding!"

"I wish I was," said Brian, as he angrily hurled a piece of wood at the woodpile.

Brenda knew just how frustrated Brian had become with this case and that this bad news would set the mood for the remainder of the day.

Tips kept coming in on suspected serial killer Calvin Knight. The media had nicknamed him "The Night

Killer," and was putting pressure on the department to catch him.

Brian was spending more and more time away from home, but being a detective he understood that sometimes that meant having to work long hours. He didn't like the idea of Brenda being home alone, but he knew he could count on Jason to look after things for him. Knowing that still didn't make him feel any less guilty, especially when Steve took every opportunity to let Brian know that it was Jason, who was spending more and more time alone with Brenda.

It was Saturday morning and the first snow of the season was slowly coming down. Brenda was feeling especially lonely as she stood in front of the kitchen window. She could hear the sound of Jason's truck coming down the road before she ever saw it. As Jason turned into the driveway, Brenda was already slipping on her coat and wrapping a scarf around her neck to go and greet him.

Jason pulled his truck up next to the barn and as he climbed out, he noticed Brenda coming out of the house. He stood there waiting for her and flashed a smile her way as she walked over to him.

"Good morning."

"Good morning," said Brenda, smiling cheerfully. "So

what does Brian have planned for you on this snowy morning?"

"Nothing that I know of, but I haven't talked to him for a few days now."

"Is there something he needs done?"

"Not that I know of, but then I really haven't seen him long enough to ask him."

Feeling awkward now, Jason said, "Well I'm sure he'd much rather be here with you then chasing after a killer."

There was a moment of awkward silence and then Jason said, "I better get the horses fed."

"I'll go with you," said Brenda, as she followed Jason into the barn.

After they had taken care of the horses, Jason went into the tact room to get his saddle. When he came out, he found Brenda sitting on a bale of straw waiting for him.

"You're going riding in the snow?" she asked.

"Yeah, I thought I'd ride out to the winter pasture and check to see how much hay is left."

"Would you mind if I ride along with you?"

Jason was surprised that Brenda wanted to go along, but deep down he was glad that she did.

"No, I don't mind," he replied.

Jason had grown very fond of Brenda and he enjoyed her company. He knew his feelings for her were growing stronger and that it wasn't right for him to have those kinds of feelings for his friend's wife, but he couldn't help himself. Since they had started spending so much time together, he hadn't been able to stop thinking about her and he looked forward to seeing her more and more every day. Brenda had asked Jason to teach her his horse training techniques. At first, he was reluctant, but when she came down every day to watch and asked if he thought his techniques would work on Hank, he slowly gave in.

Brenda turned out to be an excellent student and Jason felt a strong bond forming between them. There were days when he dreaded leaving Brenda, and he fanaticized about what it would be like to be married to her.

From the first day he met her, Jason thought Brenda had a sultry beauty about her, but it was her love of animals, sense of humor and easy smile, that attracted him the most to her. However, Jason wasn't kidding himself either. He knew how devoted she was to Brian and how much they loved one another. He had tried his best to keep his distance from her and his feelings in check, but the more he was around her, the harder it was for him to stay away.

After checking on the cattle and making sure the fence was secure, Brenda and Jason started back to the barn. They were laughing and talking when

Hank suddenly stopped and snorted. He was looking toward an opening in the woods and was refusing to move. Brenda couldn't see anything that would cause his nervousness, but suddenly she too had a very uneasy feeling.

"Come on Hank," she said in a calm voice, while trying to urge him forward.

Hank continued to stay on high alert as he began sidestepping nervously along the path.

"This isn't like him," Brenda told Jason. "He rarely gets this spooked."

"He might have seen a deer," said Jason. "There are a lot of deer tracks in this area."

"Maybe," said Brenda, with uncertainty in her voice as she looked behind them, searching for whatever had frightened Hank.

When they reached the barn and had the horses put away, Jason said, "I have to get going, but tell Brian I'll take some hay out to the cattle in the morning."

"I will... and Jason... thanks for everything you've been doing around here. I don't know how we ever would have managed without your help."

"You don't have to thank me, I should be thanking you."

"Well I better get going. I'll see you tomorrow."

Brenda flashed Jason a smile and said, "Ok, I'll see you in the morning."

Jason drove home that day feeling light hearted and guilty all at the same time.

"What the hell am I doing?!" he asked himself.

"This is crazy!"

"I can't fall in love with my best friend's wife."

It was snowing harder now, as Brenda settled in for another lonely night. Brian had called just before dinner to say he wouldn't be home until late. Brenda was tempted to call him back just so she could hear his voice, but decided she better not bother him while he was working. Going into the den, she put some wood in the fireplace. She was about to light a fire, when she suddenly paused to listen carefully to a sound that was coming from outside the house.

"What is that?" she wondered nervously. The first thought that crossed her mind was the serial killer. She walked cautiously over to the window and peeked out. It was too dark to see much, so she stood there for a moment watching and listening. When she didn't hear anything more, she went back to lighting her fire. After the fire was lit, Brenda went into the kitchen to pop herself some popcorn. As she was taking the popcorn from the microwave, she heard another noise. This time the sound was just outside the kitchen door. Brenda's pulse began to race as she hurried into the den to grab the fire poker. Cautiously heading back to the kitchen, she peeked out the window. She heard the noise again but she was still unable to see anything.

 She called out, "Who's there?" but no one answered. Brenda's heart was pounding as she called out again. "I think you should know I have a weapon and I've called the police!"

But still no one answered her.

Chapter 3

Brian was just getting into his car to head home when he received a call. Night's car had been spotted about a half mile from the ranch and several police cars were in hot pursuit. Brian quickly made a decision to join the chase. Turning on his siren and flashing lights he sped through town as he called for updates on the pursuit.

Brenda was trembling as she heard a series of thuds outside the kitchen door. To her it sounded as if someone was hitting the door with something. Terrified, Brenda reached for the phone. She was about to call 911 when she heard scratching and then what sounded like a dog whimpering.
She walked over and very carefully cracked the door open. Peering out, she saw a snow covered, half-grown puppy shivering on the other side of the door staring up at her. Brenda opened the door and the little black pup came rushing into the house. Once inside, he immediately began running in circles, jumping on Brenda and sending wet snow flying all over the kitchen floor.
"Well," said Brenda, scooping the excited puppy up in her arms, "where did you come from?"

She carried the puppy into the bathroom and set him in the tub. Grabbing a towel from the cabinet, she quickly began drying the wiggly little dog while assessing his condition.

He was quite thin and looked to be a half grown Doberman mix.

"I bet you're starving aren't you?" said Brenda. The puppy cocked his head and looked up at Brenda with his dark eyes and his one ear that stood straight up while the other was still half flopped over. Brenda's heart melted as she looked at this thin, silly looking, happy little dog.

Getting out some leftover chicken and potatoes that she had for dinner, she quickly warmed him up a bowl of food. Brenda watched as he hungrily gobbled the food up and licked the plate clean.

Brenda couldn't think of anyone in the area who had puppies, so she was at a loss as to where this puppy had come from.

"Did someone dump you off?" she asked the pup. She couldn't imagine anyone dumping a young animal out in this weather to fend for himself.

As Brenda moved around the house, the puppy stayed right by her side.

"You're like my little shadow," she told the puppy. "Maybe that's what I should name you. Shadow." As Brenda said the puppy's name, he perked up his ears and cocked his head as he looked at her.

"Ok, Shadow it is."

"Well Shadow, I wonder what Brian's going to think of you when he gets home."

Brenda sat on the floor eating her popcorn as she watched one of her favorite shows on TV.

Shadow lay next to her, resting his head on her lap while enjoying the warmth from the fire.

It was ten o'clock and Brian still wasn't home.

Brenda folded a blanket and laid it on the floor next to the bed. Before long, her and Shadow where both sound asleep.

Brian was exhausted as he walked up the steps to the house.

They had lost their suspect again and he was not in a good mood. Sliding his key into the lock, he thought he heard a dog bark. He paused for a moment before turning the key and opening the door. Trying to slip quietly into the house, Brian was suddenly greeted by a fired up, little black, barking, half-grown puppy.

"Come here Shadow!" called Brenda, as she sleepily walked into the kitchen.

"When did you get a dog?" asked a surprised Brian.

"He just showed up at our door."

"Sure he did," said a wary Brian.

"I wouldn't go out and intentionally get a puppy without talking to you first," said Brenda.

Brian let out a deep sigh as he stared at the goofy looking little dog.

"He's really sweet and he was cold and covered with snow and hungry when I found him."

"Don't look at me like that! I couldn't just leave him outside to freeze!"

Brian stood there dumbfounded as he stared at the puppy and the puppy stared back at him.

"I wonder where he came from."

"I don't know, I think someone may have dumped him out."

"He's really cute, isn't he? I'd really like to keep him if it's ok with you."

"He'd be good company for me and he'll let me know if anyone's around."

"You'll have to see if you can find his owner."

"I know," said Brenda.

"I guess it wouldn't hurt to have a dog around."

"He definitely has guard dog potential, so if we do end up keeping him he's going to need some obedience training."

"So I can keep him then?" Brenda asked excitedly.

Brian sighed as he looked from Brenda to the puppy. Bending down he called the puppy over to him.

"What's one more animal?"

"I named him Shadow because he follows me around like a little shadow."

"Well before you get too attached to him, you need

to make sure he doesn't belong to anyone else."

"I will," said Brenda, all smiles now.

Brenda put her arms around Brian's neck and gave him a kiss, as Shadow happily danced around the kitchen floor.

"Thank you sweetheart," she said.

"Look, you even made Shadow happy."

"Don't thank me yet. Someone may be looking for that silly looking rack of bones."

Jason turned his truck onto the main street of town after he left the ranch. He was heading for Darby's Bar and Grill for a sandwich and a beer before going home. He hoped having a drink would help him sleep and he wouldn't have to think about Brenda. He chose a seat at the bar and after the bartender had brought him his second beer, he felt someone hit him on the shoulder.

"Hey, Jason. What have you been up to?" asked Steve.

"Not much. How have you been Steve?"

"Good, real good. I guess you've heard that Brian and I have been chasing after that serial killer."

Jason shook his head, "Yeah, I heard. How's that going?"

"Not so good. Every time we think we have him, he manages to get away. It's just a matter a time before we nail him."

Jason never cared much for Steve and he wasn't in the mood to carry on a lengthy conversation with him, especially tonight.

They had had some heated disagreements in the past, so Jason was wondering why Steve was being so friendly all of a sudden.

"Brian says you're boarding your horse at his place now."

"That's right."

"So... what's your opinion of his wife, Brenda?" quizzed Steve.

"She seems nice."

"So you like her."

"Why wouldn't I?" asked Jason

"No reason. She is a pretty little thing, don't you think?" Steve pressed on.

Jason took a drink and tried to ignore Steve's question.

"Come on!" said Steve, nudging Jason in the ribs. "You can tell me."

 "Don't act like you haven't noticed!"

Jason sat there wondering where Steve was going with all these questions about Brenda and decided to turn the tables on him.

 "So are you telling me that you're attracted to Brian's wife?"

"Hardly! But I know a lot of guys that wouldn't mind hitting that!" replied Steve, with a smug grin on his face.

"You know what Steve? I didn't come here to talk about Brian's wife, so why don't you just let me finish my beer and go bother someone else."

"Oh come on, don't tell me you haven't wondered what it would be like to crawl on top of her!"

"You know what Steve? You're an asshole and I think you have a serious problem when it comes to women. If Brian knew you were talking that way about his wife, he'd kick your ass!"

Jason downed his beer and with a disgusted look on his face he said, "I have to go!"

"Go you lying asshole!" Steve said under his breath. "You're not kidding anyone by acting all high and mighty," spat Steve.

"What'd you say?" asked the bartender.

"Nothing," said Steve. "Just get me another beer."

On his drive home, Jason was wishing he had never stopped at Darbys. He felt guilty enough about Brenda without listening to Steve, and now he felt even worse, because he knew deep down, he had wondered what it would be like to make love to her.

It continued to snow throughout the night and by Sunday morning, four more inches of snow had fallen.

Brian went down to the barn to care for the horses because Jason still hadn't arrived by ten o'clock. It wasn't like Jason to be this late on a Saturday so Brian decided he better load up one of the large, round bales of hay and take it out to the cattle before the snow got any deeper.

By the end of the day, Jason was still a no show and both Brian and Brenda were surprised that he hadn't called to let them know he wasn't coming. Brian finally tried calling him to make sure he was all right, but he didn't answer and Brian never heard a word from him all weekend.

Monday morning, Brian and Brenda got up to find eight more inches of blowing and drifting snow on the ground, bringing the total to ten inches.

"Burr, it's cold in here," Brenda told Brian as she walked into the kitchen. "How about turning the heat up in this place before I freeze to death!"

"You're not thinking about driving to work in this are you?" Brian asked.

"Heavens no! I doubt anyone will make it in today."

"Do you have to go in?"

"Not unless I get a call saying they caught Knight."

"Good, then how about getting a fire started while I start breakfast."

"I have a better idea. Why don't we go back to bed and start a fire of our own?" suggested Brian.

"I don't know Detective, my husband may not

approve of that idea," teased Brenda.

"Well then we just won't tell him," said Brian, as he scooped Brenda up into his arms and carried her into the bedroom.

Brian laid Brenda down on the bed, kissing her tenderly. As their passion grew, Brenda whispered, "Brian, I need to,".....but Brian wasn't listening. He covered her mouth with his, and kissed her passionately. It had been a long time since they had made love and his need for her was strong as he slid his body on top of hers and kissed her breasts. He heard her moaning softly in his ear as his mouth and tongue toyed with her nipples.

"Brian, I think I should," she whispered breathlessly as Brian slid his penis into her body. He paused briefly and looked deep into her eyes as he began to thrust his body against hers. Brenda felt his passion mount as she thought about her birth control devise in the bathroom. Screw it, she thought, just this once shouldn't be a problem.

After their lovemaking, they lay in bed cradled in each other's arms. Shadow leaped on top of the bed whining and began turning in circles.

"I think he needs to go out," Brenda told Brian.

"I'll take him," said Brian.

"Come on kill joy, let's go."

When Brenda looked at the clock, she found it hard to believe that they had stayed in bed all morning.

"I'll fix lunch," she called out to Brian as he headed for the door.

Brenda was smiling as she stood in the kitchen looking out the window. She watched as Brian played in the snow with Shadow. Her smile faded when she saw Brian stop and pull his phone from his pocket. He was talking with someone as he walked back toward the house. Shadow came rushing in all excited when Brian opened the door.

"What now?" Brenda asked, looking concerned.

Brian smiled, "They finally caught him."

"They caught Night?"

"Someone spotted him hiding out in one of the hunting cabins up on Bakers Ridge and called it in. They just picked him up and they're taking him to the station now."

"Thank God!" said Brenda.

"I have to go in, but I should be back before dinner."

Brian kissed Brenda and hurried into the bedroom to change.

Winter had finally ended and it had been a beautiful spring day.

Brian had just arrived home after spending the entire day testifying at Night's trial.

Tomorrow would be the closing arguments and

then it would be up to the jury to decide the fate of Calvin Night.

During Night's testimony at the trial, he admitted that he had murdered and dumped the body of Penny Boyd just outside of Cambridge, but had maintained his innocence in regards to all of the other women.

When Brian interrogated him the night he was arrested, Night told Brian he had picked Penny up at a bar and took her to his place intending to have sex with her. When she refused his advances and wanted to leave, he said he got angry and lost it.

"She started screaming and clawing at my face so I grabbed her by the hair and dragged her out to the garage. I told her to shut up, but she just kept screaming! So I took a roll of duct tape, wrapped it around her hands and put a piece across her mouth. Then you know what that little bitch did? She kicked me in the balls! So I knocked her sorry ass down on the floor and gave it to her good!"

Brian remembered fighting the urge to reach across the table and decking Night as he told him what he had done to the young woman.

"I knew I couldn't just let her go after what I had done or she'd run straight to the police!"

"So you shot her," said Brian.

"Yeah, I shot the little tease! I shot her right in the head."

Brian recalled how Night had looked away for a moment after admitting he had killed her. He looked as if he were replaying the scene over in his mind. Then he looked back at Brian and said, "I didn't kill those other women. If I had I'll tell you." Brian hoped he was lying, but he had to wonder if he had told him the truth and there was another murderer still out there. The ballistics report on the bullets used to kill the other women, didn't match Night's gun and none of the other girls had been sexually molested.

Night could have stalked and killed those other women when they refused his advances and he could have another gun stashed somewhere. Whatever the case, the murders stopped after he was arrested and now all Brian could do was hope he had been lying and that there wasn't another killer still out there.

Brian arrived home early the following day and when he pulled into the driveway, he noticed Brenda and Jason in the round pen together, with their horses. They were both so intent on what they were doing they hadn't noticed him drive in. As he walked over to the round pen, he watched as

Brenda worked both horses in unison.
Using nothing but a long whip with a white cloth
tied to the end of it, she sent the horses in one
direction and then in one smooth gesture they
switched direction. She also had them go from a
walk to a canter, stop and walk up to her.
Brian was filled with pride as he watched his wife in
awe.
Brenda was all smiles when she finished the
exercise and gave Jason a hug.
"Ok you two, break it up," said Brian as he leaned
against the railing of the round pen watching them.
"How long have you been there?" asked a surprised
Brenda.
Delighted to see her husband home early for a
change, she hurried over to him with both horses
following close behind her.
"Long enough to notice my wife has become a horse
whisperer," said Brian. "I have to admit I'm really
impressed!"
Brenda was bursting with pride. She had been
waiting a long time to show Brian what she had
learned and she could tell she had impressed him.
"Jason deserves all the credit. He's been an excellent
teacher," said Brenda.
"I can't take all the credit. You're wife's a natural,"
said Jason, feeling uncomfortable knowing that
Brian had seen them hug.

"I can see that."

"She's been dying to show you what she's learned."

"Well I'm glad I made it home in time to watch her."

"Ok you two, you're giving me a big head," giggled Brenda.

Brian couldn't help but feel a twinge of jealously toward Jason. He wished he had been the one spending time with Brenda instead of him.

"Let me put the horses away and then I'll start dinner," said Brenda.

"I thought maybe we could go out for dinner," said Brian.

Brenda's eyes lit up as she flashed Brian a smile.

"You won't get an argument from me," she said.

The horses followed Brenda into the barn with Jason and Brian trailing along behind them.

"You don't think she's planning on training me like that do you?" Brian asked Jason.

Brian was waiting for Brenda to finish dressing when she called out, "Where are we going for dinner?"

"I thought we'd go to the Steak Barn, if that's alright with you."

"Oh good. I love that place."

Brenda remembered the first time Brian had taken

her there he taught her how to two-step.

She was hoping he'd be in the mood to dance, because it had been a long time since they had been dancing.

Brenda had slipped on a blue denim skirt and a lightweight sweater. Then she got the earrings out of the box that Brian had given her.

"Aren't those the earrings I gave you?"

"Yes. I've been wanting to wear them and I thought tonight was as good a time as any to show them off."

"Well they're beautiful, just like you."

"Have I told you lately how much I love you?" asked Brenda, as she slid her arms around Brian's neck.

Brian gave Brenda a kiss, "I love you too darling," he said.

"Are you ready? We need to get going if we don't want to lose our reservation."

"Ready," said Brenda, grabbing a jacket and her purse.

It seemed like old times as Brian and Brenda teased each other and reminisced about old times over dinner. The band started playing a slow country song and Brenda held her hand out to Brian and said, "Dance with me."

He took her hand in his and he led her to the dance floor. Pulling her close, they began to sway to the

61

music as Brenda rested her head against his chest. By their third dance, Brenda was ready to leave. "Take me home so I can have my way with you," she whispered in Brian's ear.

Brian stopped dancing and looked at his wife. Then he escorted her off the dance floor and out to the car.

When they got inside the house, Brenda pulled Brian's jacket off and shoved him up against the kitchen door. She was kissing him with such urgency that it sent his senses reeling. He kissed her neck as she pulled at his shirt, freeing it from his jeans.

She ran her hands up and down the length of his masculine chest as he slid his hands under her skirt and lifted her up to him. Wrapping her legs tightly around his hips, he carried her over to the kitchen table and pushed the flowers aside as he sat her down.

Pulling her sweater over her head and tossing it aside, he began fumbling with the hooks on her lace bra.

Brian gazed at her soft supple breasts as he ran his hands over them. He began caressing and kissing them. He ran his tongue over them before taking one in his mouth. Hearing Brenda's moans and feeling her warm body pressing against his drove him to new heights of desire. He pulled her to him and she slid her hands down the length of his body while gently biting his shoulder.

Unhooking his pants, she slid her hand down to his swollen penis and began caressing him. His breathing became rapid as she pushed his jeans down and urged him to enter her.

"Make love to me," she said. "I want you to take me right here, right now."

Brenda's body was aching to feel him inside her as she pulled his hips closer to hers.

Brian slid Brenda's panties off and pulled her against him. She watched as he slid his penis inside her, gasping as he thrust his body deep inside hers.

"Harder," she cried. "Oh, god, that feels so good."

"Yes, right there! Don't stop. Oh, yes. That's it, right there. Harder," she cried!

Brian repeatedly thrust his body against hers until he couldn't hold out any longer. He groaned as he felt the surge of passion shooting from his body into hers.

"Not yet," she cried, still clinging to him. But it was over and the aching desire inside Brenda's body went unsatisfied.

Realizing he had failed to satisfied his wife, Brian apologized.

"I'm sorry babe. I just couldn't hold out any longer."

Brenda said nothing as she released him and slowly slid from the table.

The next day Brian sat at his desk thinking about his performance and feeling guilty for not having satisfied his wife. He rarely went home for lunch on Saturday's, but today Brian thought he would surprise Brenda by picking up some flowers and taking her to lunch.

As he drove to the ranch he spotted Steve's car parked along the side of the road just down from his driveway. He pulled up next to his car and looked around. Brian was confused as to why Steve's car would be parked out there.

When Brian pulled up to the house Brenda and Jason came walking out. Brian could tell they were surprised to see him and he couldn't help but wonder why Jason was coming out of his house with his wife.

"Brian, I'm so glad you're home!" said a frantic Brenda.

"There's water running all over the kitchen floor!"

"Great!" said Brian, handing Brenda the flowers as he hurried into the house.

Brenda was right, there was water covering the kitchen floor.

"I shut the water off under the sink," said Jason. "One of the water pipes is leaking."

"I'll get my tools," said Brian.

As Brian and Jason repaired the leak, Brenda mopped up the water that was on the floor.

"I think that should do it!" said Brian.

"Thank God!" said Brenda. "What a mess!"

"I don't know what I would have done if you guys hadn't been here!"

"Thanks for your help Jason," said Brian, feeling bad now for mistrusting him.

"No problem."

"Here let me get these tools out of your way," Jason told Brenda, as he gathered up the tools and carried them out to the tool shed.

"Give me a few minutes to finish cleaning this up and I'll fix you guys some lunch," Brenda told Brian.

"Thanks babe, but I've got to get back to work. I planned on taking you out for lunch, but since this took so long to fix, I won't have time now."

"Oh, I would have loved going to lunch with you."

"Well at least let me fix you a sandwich before you go."

"Don't bother. I'll just grab something on my way back."

"Well thanks for the flowers," said Brenda, giving Brian a kiss.

"Sorry about last night," said Brian.

"So that's why you brought me flowers and wanted to take me to lunch."

"Partly, but I also wanted to spend some time with you."

"That's so sweet. No wonder I love you."

"I love you too babe. Don't ever doubt that. I have to go, but I'll see you tonight."

"See ya Jason," yelled Brian, as he headed for the car. Jason waved goodbye as Brian got into his car and drove off.

As Brian pulled out of the driveway and onto the road, it dawned on him that Steve's car was no longer there.

"What are you up to Steve?" wondered Brian, as he turned his car towards town and headed back to the station.

"That was close!" Steve told himself as he paced the floor of his apartment.

Steve had spotted Brian's car coming down the road and hid in the cornfield until Brian had left.

Damn it! Now I'm going to have to come up with some kind of explanation for why my car was parked there.

Steve was hoping that Brian had caught his wife and Jason together when he got to the house. He had watched Brenda hurrying out of the house shortly after Jason arrived and then watched as they went into the house together. He figured they were still inside the house when Brian arrived and hoped that if Brian caught them together, he'd be so upset he'd forget all about seeing his car.

When Monday morning came, Brian was busy at his desk when he looked up and noticed Steve coming through the door of the police station.

"Hey Brian," said Steve cheerfully, hoping that Brian had forgotten about seeing his car parked out by his place.

"Steve," said Brian.

Steve started to walk past Brian when he heard him say, "I noticed your car was parked along the road out by my place Saturday, but I didn't see you anywhere around. What were you doing out there?"

"I had to take a wiz so I went in the cornfield."

"You had to drive clear out by my place to take a pee? Somehow, I find that hard to believe. Why don't you try again."

Steve was nervous now, as Brian sat there staring at him, waiting to hear his explanation.

Captain Phillips came walking over and interrupted them by telling Brian there had been another murder over in Montgomery. Steve used that opportunity to quickly slip away and the next thing he knew Captain Phillips and Brian were leaving the building.

A week had passed and Jason was working out at the ranch cleaning horse's stalls, when he began to feel sick to his stomach.

It was a beautiful day and since Brenda had finished her housework, she decided it would be a good day to go horseback riding. She walked down to the barn and when she got inside, she found Jason sitting on a bale of straw, doubled over in pain. He looked pale and his forehead was perspiring.

"Jason, are you ok? What happened?"

"I don't know. I'm not feeling very well,"

"I'm sorry, but I think I better leave. Do you mind finishing up for me?"

"No I don't mind, but do you think you should be driving? You look terrible! Why don't you come up to the house so I can get my purse and then I'll drive you home," said Brenda.

"I'll be fine," said Jason. "You don't have to....."

Jason started to get up when he moaned and doubled over in pain.

"Come on, you're going up to the house with me and I'm not taking no for an answer!" said Brenda, as she helped Jason to his feet.

Brenda put her arm around Jason's waist and helped him to the house.

Steve sat crouched behind a group of trees snapping pictures, as Brenda and Jason headed for the house with their arms around one another.

"Well, well, what do you know?" he said to himself.
"Once a cheat, always a cheat! Well I can promise
you this Brenda, you're not going to get away with it
this time," he said as he snapped pictures of them
going into the house together.
"You may be able to fool your husband, but when he
sees these pictures, you'll be out of his life forever."
Steve hurried back to his car convinced that all his
suspicions about Brenda and Jason had been right
all along. Now all he had to do was figure out how to
get the pictures into Brian's hands without him
finding out who took them.

Jason hadn't been back out to the ranch for several
days, leaving Brenda to do the evening chores. As
she closed the barn door and turned toward the
house, she nearly tripped over Shadow who was
looking at the cornfield on the other side of the
driveway.
Shadow was fixated on something and as he stared
at the field, he began growling.
"What is it Shadow?"
"What do you see? Is there something out there?"
Suddenly feeling uneasy Brenda started walking
toward the house.
Shadow continued growling and then he began to
bark.

"Come on boy, let's go to the house."

"Come on Shadow!" she commanded, but he refused to follow her.

Shadow looked at Brenda for one brief second as she stood there waiting for him, before bolting for the cornfield.

"Shadow, come back here!" yelled Brenda, but he was on a dead run as he charged into the field.

Brenda watched as Shadow disappeared from sight. She called out to him and then whistled and called out again. But he didn't return.

Frightened that he would get lost, she headed for the field.

As she walked through the rows of corn, she continued calling out. She heard him bark and then she heard a rustling noise and stopped to listen. Not sure which direction the noise had come from, she called out again.

"Shadow. Come Shadow."

"Come on boy!"

Brenda's heart started to pound when she heard another rustling noise followed by a yelp and then what sounded like something or somebody, running through the corn. Suddenly everything went quiet. Brenda stood there trying to decide what she should do. She called out again, but gave up when Shadow didn't return. As Brenda climbed the porch steps, she looked back at the cornfield hoping to see

Shadow come racing out at any moment. But there was no sign of him.

The serial killer quickly jumped into his car and slammed the door. He cursed as he looked around for something to wrap around his badly bruised and bleeding arm. He was angry that he had dropped his gun, but he also felt lucky to have escaped with just an arm injury and a torn shirt.

As he sped down the road, his anger continued to mount.

"If it hadn't been for that stinking dog I'd of had her," he told himself! He knew what he needed to do.

He spun his car onto the main road and headed back into town.

CHAPTER 4

Brian was on his way home from work when he spotted Shadow limping down the road. "What in the world is he doing out here?" He asked himself, as he pulled up next to the dog and stopped.
Reaching across the seat, Brian opened the passenger's side door and called out, "Shadow, come on boy."
Shadow looked at the car and was reluctant to get in.
"Shadow! Here boy," Brian called out again.
This time Shadow recognized Brian's voice and jumped into the car. He quickly sat down on the seat and started licking Brian's face.
"Ok, settle down you big lug."
"What are you doing out here? Have you been chasing rabbits again?"
"I bet your mother doesn't know you're out here?"

Brenda was keeping a close watch out the window for Shadow when Brian pulled in. As soon as she saw him, she raced to the door to tell him that Shadow had run off and hadn't come back. Just as she walked out the door, Brian opened the car door and Shadow climbed out. Brenda gave a sigh of relief as soon as she saw him.
"Shadow, you bad boy. Where have you been?"

"I've been worried sick about you!" scolded Brenda.

"Where'd you find him?" Brenda asked Brian.

"He was coming down the road. Weren't ya, you big dope?!" Brian said affectionately.

"What's wrong with his leg?" asked Brenda, as she noticed him limp into the house.

"I don't know. He was limping when I picked him up."

Shadow flinched and tried to pull away when Brian lifted his leg to inspect his paw.

"Sorry," said Brian, when Shadow let out a yelp.

"He acts like his shoulder is bothering him."

"If he's not better in the next couple days, we should probably take him in and have the vet look him over."

"I don't know what got into him," said Brenda.

"We were coming out of the barn when he started growling and barking at something in the cornfield."

"The next thing I knew, he took off like a bolt of lightning and wouldn't come back."

"He probably spotted a deer or a raccoon in the cornfield. Dog's like to chase just about anything that'll run from them."

"Maybe," said Brenda, still not totally convinced.

"It's just not like him to refuse to come back when I call him."

"Well he's home now and I bet he's just about as hungry as I am."

"Ok, I can take a hint," said Brenda.

Jason returned to the ranch over the weekend and he and Brian were in the barn getting the horses ready to ride out and check on the cattle when Brian's phone rang. Jason could tell by the tone of Brian's voice that whatever he was being told was not good news. When Brian hung up he told Jason he was sorry but that he had to leave.

"Would you mind checking on the cattle for me?"

"No I don't mind. What's up?" asked Jason.

"A hiker just found another body in the woods by Silver Lake."

"What? How can that be, I thought the killer was in jail!"

"Yeah, well I'll know more when I get out there. Will you turn Charger back out for me? I need to get out there."

"Sure."

"And would you mind letting Brenda know what's going on?"

"No problem."

"Thanks man. I'll try and catch up with you later."

As Brian walked onto the murder scene, he noticed Max questioning the hiker that had found the woman's body. Brian walked over and noticed that the man was visibly shaken. He described seeing the young woman's leg sticking out from behind a tree along the hiking trail.

Brian walked over to the body and the first thing he noticed was that the body was that of a young dark haired woman, just as the rest of the women were. She looked like she had been shot at point blank range in the head. Her hands and feet were bound with duct tape just like all the rest. Brian swallowed as he felt his heart start to pound. He was remembering what Calvin Night had told him in the interrogation room.

"I didn't kill any of those other women. If I had I'd tell you."

Brian noticed some bruises on the woman's naked body. It looked like she had fought with her assailant before she was shot.

Because this case had the same similarities as the others, Brian was wondering if the serial killer was in fact still out there and Knight had told the truth. If he was out there, the ballistics report on the bullet would give him his answer.

When the medical examiner arrived and turned the body over, Brian realized he had seen this young woman before.

"I know her!" said Brian.

Surprised, Steve said, "You know this girl?"

"She was a waitress at the Country Barn Steak Barn."
"She waited on Brenda and I the last time we were
there. I think her name was Sharon or Sherry."
Steve stared at Brian and then at the young woman
as Brian told the other officers, "Make sure you
check every square inch of this area, we don't want
to miss anything!"
"I think we better drive out to the Steak Barn and
see what we can find out about this girl," Brian told
Steve.
"Sure thing," replied Steve.
As they started toward their vehicles one of the
officers yelled, "Hey Brian, you might want to take a
look at this!"
Brian and Steve hurried over to the officer. Lying on
the ground at the officers feet were some photos.
Brian bent down and spread the pictures out with
his pen.
"What do you make of it?" asked the officer, knowing
full well their implications.
Brian was dumbfounded as he stared at the
snapshots that were lying on the ground at his feet.
They were photos of Brenda and Jason with their
arms around one another.
"It looks like our killer may be keeping an eye on
your wife!" suggested the officer.
Brian was speechless as he put on a glove and
picked up the pictures.

Slipping them into a bag he handed them to the officer and said, "Have these checked out for fingerprints. I want to know the type of camera used and anything else you can come up with!"

"You got it!" said the officer.

Brian walked to his car with a very disturbed look on his face. Steve had never seen Brian look that way before.

"Are you ok partner?"

Brian didn't answer. He climbed into his car, shut the door and sped away, leaving Steve rushing after him.

All kinds of things were racing through Brian's head as he drove to the Steak Barn. Once there, he began questioning the bartender and discovered the victim's name was Sharon Riker. Everyone was shocked when they heard that she had been murdered.

"Do you know if she was seeing anyone or had any enemies?" asked Brian.

The bartender told Brian she was well liked and he didn't think she was seeing anyone.

"There was a man who came in on a regular basis and he always made it a point to sit at one of her tables."

"She mentioned she liked waiting on him because he was a big tipper, but I don't believe she ever went out with him."

"Do you recall if he ever stayed until her shift ended?" asked Brian.

"No, but now that you mentioned it, I did overhear her telling Carol that he had asked her what time she got off work."

"When was the last time he was in here?" asked Steve.

"Last night," replied the bartender.

"Did Miss Riker wait on him last night?" asked Brian.

"No…, come to think of it she didn't. Carol covered his table last night."

"Is Carol working today?"

"She comes in at seven."

"Did you happen to notice what time the guy left last night?" asked Brian.

"No, I didn't. It was pretty crazy in here last night."

"She didn't happen to mention the guy's name to you did she?"

"Let me think…. I believe she said his name was Jerry, but that's all I remember. You know single girls, there always talking about guys."

"I'll need to see your surveillance tapes from last night," said Brian.

"Sure, follow me."

The bartender took Brian to the back room where the tapes were kept.

"I'll need you to point this guy out to me," said Brian.

"Sure, no problem," said the bartender.

Finally the bartender said, "There he is. That's the guy right there."

"Do you mind if I take this with me?" Brian asked.

"No, be my guest."

"I'll be back later to talk to your waitresses."

"Whatever you need to do detective."

Brian's neck was aching as he sat at his desk. He couldn't get the pictures of Brenda and Jason out of his mind as he tried to concentrate on the surveillance tape.

Sgt. Max Slone, walked over to him and asked, "Hey Brian, are you ok?"

"Yeah," replied Brian, as he rubbed the back of his neck.

"This case is really getting to me and now it looks like this killer has been watching my wife."

"You know my wife and Jason. Do you think something's going on between them?"

"I wouldn't go jump to any conclusions. Why don't you just go home and talk to her. If anything turns up I'll call you."

"I think I will run home for a while. Call if you hear anything from the lab."

"Will do, and Brian. Good luck."

When Brian pulled in, Brenda was just coming out of the barn. She was surprised when she saw Brian getting out of his car. Smiling, she hurried over to greet him.

"I didn't expect you back this early," she said happily.

"We need to talk!" said Brian, in a serious voice.

"Alright. What's up?" asked Brenda, her smile suddenly fading as she looked at Brian's sober face.

"When I was out at the scene this morning, one of the officers discovered something that was pretty disturbing!" replied Brian.

Brian noticed Jason coming out of the barn, and said, "Let's go inside and talk."

When they got inside, Brenda walked over to the sink and began washing her hands, "So what did he find?" she asked, turning to look at Brian.

Brenda noticed Brian staring out the kitchen window. She turned to see what he was looking at and noticed Jason looking up at the house as he walked back into the barn.

"Brian...What did he find?" she asked.

"Pictures!"

"Pictures? What kind of pictures?"

"Pictures of you and Jason with your arms around one another. You were going into the house! This house! Our house!"

Brenda, stood there in shock.

Confused, she wondered if she had heard him right. "That's impossible!" she finally said.

"I don't believe it!"

"I couldn't believe it either, but I saw them with my own two eyes!"

"Would you like to tell me what the hell's been going on around here while I'm at work?" he demanded!

"Nothing! I swear!" said Brenda, who was hurt and angry to think Brian would accuse her of such a thing!

"I can't believe you! Do you really think... You do don't you?"

"I can't believe it!" cried Brenda, as she stared in disbelief at Brian.

Brian stood there staring back at Brenda. He wanted to believe nothing was going on, but those pictures were burned into his mind.

"Well let me make this perfectly clear! Nothing is going on between us! So you can stop looking at me like I'm some kind of criminal!" she shouted.

"I want to see these so called pictures!" she demanded.

"You can't. They're being held as evidence."

"Evidence! Evidence of what?"

"That Jason and I killed that woman?"

"Don't be silly!"

"What then?" Brenda said angrily.

"It seems whoever killed that girl may be keeping his eye on you."

"We're checking the pictures for fingerprints."

Brenda still hurt and numb didn't hear Brian say that she was being watched.

"Well, I don't know what else I can say. I thought you knew me, but I guess I was wrong!"

Tears welled up in Brenda's eyes as she turned her back to Brian and headed for the bedroom.

"Brenda, I'm sorry, but right now I don't know what to think. All I know is that creep had pictures of you and that means he's been here watching you. Your safety is all that's important right now."

Brenda slammed the bedroom door, flung herself on the bed and began to cry.

"I don't want you going out of this house unless I'm here and I don't want you letting anyone in!"

"You mean you don't want me letting Jason in!" she shouted back at him.

"No, I mean I don't want you to let anyone in!"

Brian stood there staring at the bedroom door.

Finally he said, "I'll take care of the horses from now on. I just want you to promise me you'll stay inside and keep the doors locked."

Brenda was so angry now she was only half listening.

"I'm going to go have a talk with Jason."

Not getting a response Brian said, "I'll be home before dark. Remember what I said, keep the doors locked and stay inside!"

Brian opened the door to go out when he heard

Brenda yell, "Brian!... Nothing's going on between Jason and me, so don't go accusing Jason of something that's only happening in your head!" Brian walked out the door then, slamming it behind him.

When Brenda heard the door slam she came out of the bedroom and sat at the kitchen table until she heard Brian's car start up and drive away. She suddenly felt sick to her stomach as she went back to the bedroom and flung herself onto the bed. She began crying as Brian's angry words ran through her head.

This had been the second time today she had felt like she was going to thrown up. She hadn't felt well all morning and now that her life seemed to be turning upside down, she felt even worse.

Lying on the bed, Brenda felt as if her head was about to explode when she heard the phone ring.

"Hello?" said Brenda, in a drab voice.

"Hi sis. You sound terrible! Is everything ok?" asked Julie, Brenda's sister.

"I'm just having a bad day," said Brenda, sounding tired.

"What's going on?"

Brenda started to cry, "Everything's such a mess!"

"Another body was found this morning and Brian came home and accused me of having an affair with Jason because of some pictures that were found at the crime scene," she sobbed.

"Whoa...What? Run that by me again!"

"Brian was called out to a crime scene and apparently one of his officers found some pictures of Jason and I. Brian claims we had our arms around one another and we were coming in the house."

"These pictures were found at the crime scene?"

"That's what he said!"

"That's really strange...and scary!"

"Didn't you hear what I said! Brian thinks I'm having an affair with Jason and it's just not true!"

There was a long silence before Julie finally said, "Why would you have your arms around one another?"

"We wouldn't! That's just it! It makes no sense!" replied Brenda.

"Well if he has pictures...."

"Don't you start! I swear, doesn't anyone believe me?" cried Brenda.

"Sorry, I didn't mean to make it sound like I thought you were doing something wrong. What bothers me is some crazy serial killer has been at the ranch watching you, not what those pictures look like! That's really scary Sis!"

"I know that, but right now I'm more worried about what Brian's thinking! I would never cheat on him Julie!"

"I know you wouldn't. I'm just surprised Brian hasn't realized it by now."

"So you can't think of any time that you and Jason were walking up to the house, for whatever reason, with your arms around each other?"

"No!" said Brenda, trying to think back.

"Well now that I think about it, I did have my arm around him the day I had to help him to the house when I found him doubled over in pain in the barn."

"I helped him to the house so I could get my purse because I didn't think he was in any shape to drive home."

"I wanted to call the doctor but he wouldn't let me."

"What was wrong with him?"

"Somehow he had gotten food poisoning."

"Julie, don't you see, that's it! That has to be when those pictures were taken! I need to call Brian."

"Brenda. Hold on a minute. If the killer is watching you, I don't want to scare you, but you could be in danger!" said Julie, now frightened for her sister's safety.

"Maybe you should talk to Brian about getting you a gun."

"A gun? You know I don't like guns. Besides, Brian has a gun and Shadow wouldn't let anyone hurt me."

"Shadow," said Brenda thoughtfully. Suddenly it dawned on her that Shadow may have chased after the killer the day he ran into the cornfield.

"Julie, can I call you later? I really need to talk to Brian."

"Ok, but don't forget to call me and be careful!"

"I will and thanks."

Brenda quickly hung up and called Brian's office.

"That had to be really rough seeing those pictures of Jason and Brenda with their arms around one another," said Steve.

"None of this makes any sense," said Brian.

"Brenda's never given me any reason to believe she'd cheat on me and I could tell she was really upset when I practically accused her of having an affair with Jason."

"You didn't really expect her to admit it did you?"

"I don't know what I expected. I just know Brenda's never lied to me before and when I spoke to Jason he was equally upset when I told him about finding those pictures."

"I bet he was," said Steve.

"You have been gone a lot lately. Brenda probably got lonesome and I warned you about Jason and women. It's like I've always said, you can't trust any of these women anymore!"

"What do you say we get out of here and I'll buy us a beer?"

"I don't know," said Brian. "I really don't feel like going anywhere."

"Oh, come on. It'll be like old times. Besides, you look like you could use a beer or two."

As Brian and Steve walked out of the station, the phone on Brian's desk began to ring.

"Detective Slone. How can I help you?"

"Max? This is Brenda. Is Brian there?"

"Hi Brenda. No, I think he just left."

"Oh… Well do you know if he's on his way home?"

"I couldn't say. Is there something I can help you with?"

"No, I'm afraid not. I guess it'll just have to wait until he gets here, but thanks anyways."

"Sorry I couldn't be more help, but it was good talking to you Brenda."

"You too Max. Have a good night."

Brian was deep in thought as he finished his first beer. The longer he sat there listening to Steve talk about how useless women are, the more Brian wished he had just gone home.

"This was a bad idea," Brian finally told Steve. "I'm going to go."

"What do you mean? This is just like old times. Just you and me hanging out, drinking a beer together. You have to admit, it's better than sitting at home arguing with your old lady! You just need to loosen up. You deserve a night out!"

"Maybe, but I'm still leaving," said Brian. "Brenda was pretty upset when I left."

"I bet she was! She probably never thought she'd get caught screwing around with Jason."

"Knock it off Steve. She's still my wife and I'm still not convinced anything's going on between them."

"You've got to be kidding me! What about those pictures? Good god man, what's it going to take to wake you up!"

"Those pictures don't necessarily prove anything!"

"I have to go. Thanks for the beer. I'll see you tomorrow."

Steve couldn't believe his ears. He thought for sure, planting those pictures would have been all it would take, for Brian to see the truth about Brenda and Jason.

"What's it going to take Brian, before you discover that all women are nothing but lying little bitches that can't be trusted?"

Brenda was still waiting up to talk to Brian when he came walking through the door.

He was quiet and withdrawn as he looked at her. Brenda had never seen him like this before and it made her nervous. She had to convince him that she and Jason were innocent.

"We need to talk?" she said in a timid voice.

"What is it Brenda?"

"I think I figured out when those pictures were

taken."

Brian turned his back and started to walk away, convinced she was going to lie to him.

"Brian please, hear me out," she begged.

Brian turned around and looked her straight in the eye.

"You just suddenly figured it out!"

"Alright then. Let's hear it?" he said angrily.

"Remember when Jason had that food poisoning?"

"What about it?"

"Well don't you remember I told you I went to the barn and found him in so much pain I had to help him stand up?"

"Yeah, what about it?"

"Well I had put my arm around him to help him get to the house."

"Don't you remember? I told you I wanted to call his doctor but he wouldn't let me, so I got my purse and drove him home. We were only in here a few minutes."

"Don't you see? That had to be when those pictures were taken!"

Brian remained silent as he thought about what Brenda was saying.

"And remember the night you found Shadow on the road? I told you he heard or saw something in the cornfield and you thought it was a deer. Well he was growling at something before he took off and I've never heard him growl at a deer or any other animal before! Don't you see? He could have seen the person that was taking those pictures and went after him."

Brian ran his hand through his hair, "Well if that's true, then that's all the more reason for you to stay in this house when you're here alone."

"So do you believe me now? Because I swear to you, nothing is going on between Jason and I."

Brenda walked over and put her arms around Brian. "Why would I look at anyone else when I have you?" she said.

Brian let out a deep sigh. Brenda's story seemed to make sense and he desperately wanted to believe her.

Brian knew it wasn't in Brenda's nature to lie, so he felt certain that he had misjudged her and Jason.

Feeling relieved, he said, "Ok babe, I believe you and I'm sorry for doubting you. I guess it was just the shock of seeing those pictures."

Brian gave his wife a kiss and said, "Can you ever forgive me for doubting you?"

"I guess, but don't let it happen again!" said Brenda. They gave each other a long tender kiss and then Brenda said, "Want to have make-up sex?"

Brian looked at Brenda for a moment wondering if she was serious or just pulling his leg.

"Ok, but we'll have to make it fast because I have a

date with a very sexy brunette."

Brenda smiled and said, "Well then, I guess we better get a move on."

Brian scooped Brenda up into his arms and carried her to the bedroom.

When Brian arrived home late the following evening, he laid in bed unable to fall asleep. He looked over at Brenda who was sleeping peacefully next to him. He was concerned for her safety more than ever now, and to make things worse, her sister would be arriving in the morning and that meant he'd have one more person to worry about.

He didn't know if he would ever be able to rest knowing a killer was out there watching his wife.

Brian got up and looked out the window.

"Where are you, you sick bastard?"

"If it's the last thing I do, I'm going to find you!"

Chapter 5

 The following morning Brian was up early.
His first priority of the day was to make sure Brenda
remained safe, so as he walked to the barn he placed
a call into the station and requested a patrol car be
sent out to keep an eye on the place until he got
home.
 Brenda, unaware that Brian hadn't slept all night,
got up and checked the driveway to see if he had
gone into work.
She noticed the lights were on in the barn so she
rushed around and got dressed. By the time Brian
came up from the barn, she had breakfast all ready
and a cup of coffee sitting on the table for him.
 When they finished their breakfast, Brian said, "I'll
be home early tonight and then I'm taking you to the
shooting range so I can teach you how to use a hand
gun."
"You know I'm not comfortable around guns. They
scare me."
"Never the less we're going anyways. You'll need to
take one of their gun safety classes so you can get a
permit."
"Why would I have to take a gun safety class when I
don't have a gun?"

"Because I'm going to get you one. With everything that's going on around here you should have some way to protect yourself!"

"Isn't that what you're for?"

"Well unfortunately, I'm not always around."

"That may be true but just remember, if I go and shoot my foot off, it'll be your fault for making me do this."

"You're not going to shoot your foot off! Are you ready to go?"

"Just let me grab my purse and then I'll be ready."

Brenda backed her car out of the garage and noticed that Brian was sitting in his car waiting for her to leave. He rolled down his window and shouted, "I'll see you after work and if you get home from work before I do, stay in the house and keep the doors locked!"

"I will!"

Good grief! How many times does he think he has to tell me that, thought Brenda.

That afternoon as Brenda was returning home, she noticed a car sitting near the entrance of their driveway. Please let Brian be home, she told herself as she approached the car. Fear began racing through her veins as she looked at the driver sitting in the car.

"Oh thank god, it's only Steve!" Brenda said to herself. Brenda let out a sigh of relief. She had to admit that she did feel better knowing someone was there keeping an eye on the place, even if it was Steve.

 Brenda waved as she turned in the driveway and headed toward the house. Steve nodded as she passed him and then fell in behind her.

Brenda pulling her car into the garage and then went straight into the house, closing the garage door behind her. As she laid her purse on the table, she heard a knock at the door. Looking out the kitchen window, she noticed Steve waving his hand for her to open the door.

 Brenda unlocked the door and as she opened it Shadow rushed to her side and began growling at Steve and showing his teeth. Brenda had never seen Shadow act like that toward anyone before.

"Shadow stop it! It's ok."

 Steve started to come in when Shadow lunged at him. Brenda quickly grabbed his collar to prevent him from biting Steve.

"I'm sorry Steve," said Brenda, shocked by Shadow's sudden aggressive behavior.

"I've never seen him act like this before."

Steve glared at the dog, as Shadow continued to growl and show his teeth.

"You better hope that animal never bites anyone or

he'll have to be put down."

"What do you want Steve?"

"I just wanted to tell you that you should probably let me check out the house before you go inside. Brian seems to think our killer's targeting you and he wants to make sure you're kept safe."

"Well as you can see, Shadow wouldn't let anyone in that he doesn't know."

"Maybe so, but to be on the safe side, it would still be a good idea to check things out first. Besides this guy has a gun and it only takes one bullet to stop a dog."

"How'd you talk Brian into getting a mutt like that anyway?"

"He's not a mutt! And for your information, it didn't take much persuading at all."

Steve looked at the dog with distain as Shadow kept a watchful eye on his every move.

"Oh good, here comes Brian now," said Brenda, relieved to see him come pulling in.

Steve always seemed to be able to rub Brenda the wrong way, and today was no exception.

Brenda had no problem getting along with all of Brian's other friends, but when it came to Steve, she just couldn't bring herself to like him.

Steve turned to greet Brian and Shadow lunged at him.

Brenda, still holding firmly onto Shadow's collar,

quickly pulled him inside and shut the door.

"Shadow, what has gotten into you? I know Steve's not one of my favorite people but that doesn't mean you can attack him!"

As soon as Brenda released her grip on Shadow's collar, he went straight to the window and started barking and growling at Steve.

"Thanks for coming out and keeping an eye on the place for me," said Brian.

"No problem. You know you really ought to think about getting rid of that dog. He's going to bite someone one of these days."

"Shadow? Brenda would probably get rid of me before she'd ever part with that dog," joked Brian.

"Really? That stupid mutt means more to her then you do?"

"I was just kidding Steve!"

"You sure about that?"

"Yeah, I'm sure!"

"Well I better get going," said Steve. "I'll see you tomorrow."

"Thanks again," said Brian, wondering what was eating at Steve.

That evening, Brenda felt her heart begin to race as she and Brian pulled into the shooting range.

"Are you sure you want me to do this?" she asked.

"You'll do fine. Stop worrying!"

"I know I told you that I thought carrying a gun was sexy, but I was referring to you, not me!"

"Will you stop worrying? I'll make sure you get a gun that's easy to shoot."

"Oh thanks honey, that makes me feel a lot better."

"I can hardly wait to learn how to kill a little piece of paper, because I'm pretty sure that's the only thing I'll be shooting at!"

Brian let out a sigh and shook his head.

"Come on," he said, as he opened his truck door.

Brenda looked at all the handguns that were displayed in the glass case in front of her. Feeling overwhelmed, she looked at Brian nervously.

"I'd like to see some revolvers for my wife," Brian told the owner.

After handling a number of different handguns and having Brian and the owner explain the differences, Brian asked Brenda, "So what do you think? Is there one you like?"

Brian watched as Brenda looked at the revolvers lying in front of her.

"Well out of all of them, I guess this one feels the best," replied Brenda.

"We'll take that one," Brian told the owner.

"I think you'll be happy with that one," the owner told Brenda.

"You'll have to fill out some paperwork for a gun permit and take a gun safety course before I can let you take it home." The owner informed Brenda.

"Yes, I know. My husband already explained that to me."

When Brenda was finished with the paperwork, Brian said, "Ok, let's go to the shooting range so you can get used to handling your gun."

Brenda's heart began to pound nervously as she followed Brian into the gun range.

On their drive home, Brenda said, "I didn't do very well did I?"

"You just need some more practice. You did alright for your first time," he said gently as he slid his hand onto her leg.

"I hope I didn't embarrass you too much."

"You didn't embarrass me."

"Well at least now I know if I ever do need to shoot at someone, I better not be standing too far away from them!"

Brian smiled, "You weren't that bad."

"Really? Then why did you keep saying, your target's the one in front of you," asked Brenda, trying to imitate Brian's voice.

"I never said that! And I know I didn't sound like that."

"Oh yes you did."

"We'll practice some more when you get your gun."

"Don't worry, you'll get better."

Brenda gave Brian one of her looks and said, "If you say so."

That night Brenda had a dream that the serial killer was chasing her through a forest. Terrified, she ran gripping her gun tightly in her hand. As she ran, she tripped over a limb and fell to the ground. She turned to see the killer running toward her holding a gun in his hand. She lifted her gun and pulled the trigger. The gun made a loud bang as the bullet flew from the barrel and hit and killed a bird that was sitting in a tree. Alarmed and frightened, she quickly aimed the gun again and pulled the trigger. The bullet ricocheted off a large rock, hitting the man in the leg. As he fell to the ground, Brenda suddenly woke up. Shaken, she quickly looked over at Brian who was sleeping peacefully next to her. As she lay there thinking about her dream, she concluded that if she ever had to shoot someone, there had better be a big rock close by.

After Brenda had finished her gun safety class, she picked up her gun and drove straight home.

Taking a deep breath she said, "Ok, I guess I should load this bad boy."

When she had finished, she put the safety on and

carried the gun into the bedroom, tucking it safely away in the nightstand next to the bed.

It was now Wednesday and Brenda's day off. But instead of sleeping in, she got up early so she could spend a little extra time with Brian before he left for work.

As they finished feeding the horses and were walking back to the house, Brian told Brenda that Jason would be there around ten o'clock.

"I want you to promise me you'll stay inside until he gets here," said Brian!

"Stop worrying! I have a gun now, remember?"

"Yeah, well I still want you to stay inside and keep the doors locked. I know this isn't any fun for you, but sooner or later we'll catch this guy and everything can get back to normal."

"Alright already. Good lord, I feel like a prisoner in my own house."

While Brenda was waiting for Jason to arrive, she picked up the phone and called her sister.

"It's about time you called me back," said Julie.

"Sorry, it's been really crazy around here lately."

"Brian bought a gun, and then I had to take a gun safety class so I wouldn't shoot myself, and now he's dragging me down to the shooting range three times a week to try and teach me how to shoot the thing!"

"All right then. So tell me, what happened with the pictures they found?"

"Did Brian believe you when you told him about helping Jason to the house?"

"After I explained everything to him he did."

"So everything's fine now?"

"You've made up?"

"Yes, everything's fine, except Brian has suddenly become this overly protective husband now."

"I'm really glad he believed you. So everything's good between the two of you?"

"Yup, we're all back to normal."

"Good, because I have a favor to ask of you."

"Sure. What is it?"

"I was wondering if it would be alright with you and Brian if I came and stayed with you for a while."

"Of course it's ok. Is everything alright?"

"Not really. Mike and I are having some problems and I just feel it would be better if we spent some time apart for a while."

"I'll explain everything when I get there," said Julie.

"I'm sorry. Here I am rattling on about a gun. Are you ok?"

"I'll be fine. I just need to get out of here for awhile."

"So when did you want to come?"

"Would tomorrow be too soon?"

"No, of course not. I'll let Brian know your coming when he gets home tonight."

"You're sure it'll be ok with him?"

"I'm sure and I'm really sorry about you and Mike."

"I'll see you sometime tomorrow then," said Julie.

"Ok...I can't wait to see you. Drive careful and call me when you're getting close, but I should be home from work before you get here."

"I will and thanks again sis."

"No problem. Love you."

"Love you too."

Brenda sat there for a moment wondering what could have happened that would cause Julie to leave her home and Mike. They always seemed to be so happy and in love, the perfect couple. Brenda hoped the problem wasn't because Julie hadn't been able to give Mike any children.

When Jason arrived later that morning, Brenda waved for him to come up to the house. Jason was apprehensive about being seen going to the house, even though Brian had called and apologized to him.

Brenda stood on the porch waiting for him as Shadow ran down the step to eagerly greet him. As they reached the porch steps Jason stopped.

"I just wanted to let you know how sorry I am about everything that happened. I don't want you to feel weird about being here and I know Brian wouldn't want you to feel that way either."

Jason stood there looking off into the distance. He didn't reply and Brenda could tell that whatever Brian had said, was still bothering him.

"Neither of us did anything wrong Jason, so there's no reason why things can't go back to normal. I really hope we can all get past this and stay friends."

"I just don't want to cause any more trouble between you and Brian. Both of you have been really good to me and I think the less time you and I spend together the better it'll be for everyone."

Jason turned to head for the barn when Brenda said, "Well it won't be better for me!"

"Jason please. I know Brian's sorry for accusing us of...well you know, but I also know he doesn't want us to feel uncomfortable around one another either. He really does feel bad and you've been so much help to us we'd hate to lose you."

"Brenda, I really don't want to get into this with you right now."

"You know just because some sick-o out there was spying on us, or me, doesn't mean we should let him destroy our friendship does it?"

"Brenda I know Brian's sorry. He called me and apologized for everything right after you explained everything to him."

"Then we're ok?"

"We can all still be friends?"

"It's not that I don't want to be your friend Brenda!"

"Then what is it?"

"It's just that...."Jason suddenly stopped himself from saying anything more. He wanted to tell Brenda it was because he was falling in love with her, and that being around her was tearing him apart, but he knew once he said it, he'd never be able to take it back.

"It's just what? I don't understand."

"I stand by what I said!"

Brenda stood there staring at Jason as he walked away. She didn't understand his sudden attitude, and despite what he said, she wasn't about to accept the fact that they couldn't still be friends.

Jason noticed Brenda sweeping off the porch and rode over to her.

"Will you be alright staying here by yourself while I go out and fix the fence in the back pasture?"

"Sure. I promised Brian I'd stay in the house when no one was around."

"Well I'll get going then."

Jason turned to go and as Brenda opened the door to go inside, she heard Jason shout, "Lock the door!"

"I will!" she shouted back, flashing him a smile.

"He's starting to sound just like Brian," she told Shadow, as she watched Jason disappear from sight.

Shortly after Jason returned, Brenda headed down

to the barn to find him. She wasn't about to let him off the hook that easily. While Jason was gone, Brenda devised a plan to make him see that there was no reason they couldn't remain friends.

"Would you have time to help me with something?" Brenda asked Jason as he hammered away on an old tractor behind the barn.
"What do you need?"
"I need a target set up."
Puzzled, Jason asked, "What kind of a target?"
"Well Brian insisted on buying me a gun so I can defend myself. The only problem is, I'm a terrible shot. So, I was wondering if you would help me set up some kind of a target so I can practice shooting at these," said Brenda, holding up some paper bulls-eyes she drawn.
Jason stood there stunned for a moment, as he looked at the large pieces of paper Brenda was holding in her hand.
"Wow, I don't think I've ever seen any bulls-eyes quite that large before!" he said.
"I guess I can get something set up for you. Just let me get some bales of straw and a piece of plywood from the barn and I'll see what I can come up with."
"I'm not a very good shot, so make sure it's set up far enough away from anything I could accidently kill."
"Don't worry I will!" chuckled Jason, as he headed

for the barn.

As Jason was setting up the target, Brenda went inside and came back with her handgun, a box of ammunition and Shadow, trailing behind her.

Jason tacked one of Brenda's targets to the plywood and walked back to her.

She took a deep breath as she looked at the target. "I had a dream last night," she told Jason, "that the serial killer was chasing me through the woods. He had a gun in his hand so I shot at him. But instead of hitting him, I ended up killing a bird and injuring a rock, so if I were you, I'd stand back."

Jason raised an eyebrow and took a few steps backwards.

Brenda took the safety off her revolver, aimed and pulled the trigger, totally missing the target.

Shadow jumped when he heard the gun go off and hid behind Jason's legs.

Jason stepped forward and positioned his body in a shooting stance.

"Maybe it'll help if you try standing like this. It'll give you more stability."

"Like this?" asked Brenda, as she shifted her body to match Jason's.

"That's right and try squeezing the trigger with this part of your finger. It makes it a little easier to pull the trigger back, especially if you don't have time to cock your gun."

"Ok, I'll give it a try."

Brenda took a deep breath as she tried to remember everything Brian and Jason had told her.

Brenda aimed and pulled the trigger.

Lowering her gun, she looked at the target.

"Well at least you hit the plywood that time," said Jason.

"I did?" Where?"

"In the upper right hand corner, next to that large piece of paper you call a target."

"Very funny!" said Brenda, smiling jokingly.

"Maybe I should get a little bit closer."

"I think you're close enough! Look, try pointing the barrel of the gun at the target as if you're pointing your finger at someone."

Brenda, looking discouraged, took her stance again and held her breath. Lifting the gun she cocked and aimed it at the target and pulled the trigger.

Shadow peeked around Jason's legs and then ducked back behind him.

"That was better," said Jason, giving Shadow a reassuring pat on the head.

Brenda looked at the target and was surprised to see that her bullet had actually hit the outside corner of the paper.

"What's going on out here?"

Surprised, Brenda and Jason turned to see Shadow rushing to greet Brian.

"Look honey, I hit the target!" Brenda said excitedly.

"So I see," said Brian, squinting to see the bullet hole that was nowhere near the big circle on the paper. "Hey Jason."

"Brian."

"I was just trying to give Brenda a few pointers. I hope you don't mind."

"No, I don't mind. By the looks of things she can use a few pointers."

"Well now that you're here, I'll go back and finish working on that tractor."

"You don't have to rush off," said Brian.

"You don't mind that I set this target up out here do you?" asked Jason.

"No, I don't mind and by the looks of things it's a good thing you stayed and kept your eye on her," Brian said in a low voice, thinking Brenda couldn't hear him.

"Watch it!" said Brenda.

"You know I can hear you, right? And don't forget I'm holding a deadly weapon in my hand."

"Yes I can see that," said Brian, "and if you'll take a look down you'll notice you have it pointed right at your foot!"

Brenda looked and quickly pointed the gun away from her toes.

Embarrassed now Brenda said, "If you remember

darling, I warned you that I might shoot my foot off, but you still insisted on getting me this gun."

"Yes, I do remember that," Brian said with a grin. "You know I'm only out here doing this because I wanted to surprise you."

"Sorry honey, I didn't mean to hurt your feelings."

"Why don't you try again?"

Brenda shot Brian one of her looks and then took her stance and pointed the gun at the target.

Lowering her weapon she said, "Now I'm too nervous to shoot!"

"Why are you nervous?" asked Brian.

"Because you're standing here watching me!"

"Don't be nervous."

"I promise I won't say another word."

Brenda took a deep breath and then let it out.

Aiming the gun she pulled the trigger, missing the target all together.

Brenda looked at Brian with a defeated look on her face.

"I give up," she said. "I'm just not good at this."

"Just take a couple of deep breaths and relax."

The only way you're going to get any better is to keep trying."

"I thought you weren't going to say another word!" said Brenda, biting her lower lip as she stared at the target.

"Just try squeezing the trigger a little slower,"

suggested Brian.

Brenda took another deep breath and aimed the gun at the target again.

Determined now, Brenda clenched her teeth and pulled the trigger.

"I hit it," she said, shocked that she had actually hit the circle on the paper.

Brian and Jason looked at each other and smiled. Confident now, Brenda aimed the gun again and pulled the trigger, hitting the target two more times.

"I think you're getting the hang of it," said Brian. "Just a little more practice and you'll be shooting better than me."

"Yeah, right!" scoffed Brenda. "I'll just be happy when I can come close to hitting that huge black circle I put in the center!"

Brian and Jason looked at each other again and then at Brenda and smiled.

When Brenda noticed their amusement at her expense, she said, "Alright you two, I'm out of here." "I think I've entertained you guys enough for today!"

"Don't forget to put the safety on your gun," said Brian.

Brenda turned and gave Brian one of her not so pleasant looks, and said, "I already did."

As soon as she was out of Brian's sight she quickly flipped the safety on. Looking at Shadow she said, "Don't you dare say a thing!"

Brian and Jason were finishing the evening chores when Brian asked Jason if he'd like to stay for dinner.

"Thanks but I can't," said Jason. "I have a date and I'm already running a little late."

"Anyone I know?" asked Brian.

"I don't think so. Her name's Carol Dryer, she's one of the waitresses at the Steak Barn."

"How long have you been seeing her?"

Jason opened his truck door and said, "This is our first date and if I don't get going, it might be my last."

"Well don't let me hold you up."

" I'll be here first thing in the morning to do chores."

"Don't worry about it. I'll go ahead and do them when I get up. I thought we could ride out and tag those calves when you get here.

Jason climbed into his truck and said, "Ok, I'll see you around nine o'clock then."

"Have fun tonight and don't do anything I wouldn't do."

Jason smiled as he put his truck in reverse, waved goodbye and drove away.

Brian went to the house and when he walked inside, he found Brenda waiting for him in a skimpy little red negligee.'

"Well hello there beautiful. Does my wife know you're here?"

"Of course she does, but it's ok, I have her tied up in the den.

"Do you like it?" asked Brenda, turning slowly in a circle so Brian could get a good look at her.

"What do you think?" said Brian, as he swept her up into his arms and carried her into the bedroom.

Brian laid Brenda down on the bed and gave her a kiss. "I'm going to jump in the shower. Don't move! I'll be right back."

Quickly stripping off his clothes, Brian stepped into the shower. He had just lathered up when he heard the shower door opening behind him.

Brenda stepped inside still wearing her negligee'. Running her hands down the length of his muscular body, she kissed him deeply. She stepped back as he reached for her and her dark eyes were filled with lust as they looked at one another. She began kissing and caressing his body as he slid the straps of her negligee' off her shoulders. She went down on him and he let out a moan, as her hands and her mouth drew the passion from his body.

They lay on the bed making love for a second time when Brenda heard the buzzer go off on the oven. "Dinner's ready," she said breathlessly, when they had finished.

Giving Brian one last peck on the lips she pulled on

her robe and headed for the bathroom.

Brian laid there thinking how lucky he was to have found a woman like Brenda for his wife.

"Something smells really good," said Brian, as he walked into the kitchen.

"I sure hope it tastes better than you shoot," he teased.

"That was cruel," said Brenda, picking up her oven mitt and throwing it at Brian's head.

Shadow jumped up and looked at Brenda as if she meant to hit him with the mitt.

Brian chuckling said, "That's right Shadow, you better duck. She not any better of a shot with that then she is with a gun!"

Brenda had started setting the table when she suddenly remembered her sister's phone call.

"Oh, I almost forgot to tell you. My sister's coming to stay with us for a while. It seems she and Mike are having some problems and she asked if it would be alright if she came here and stayed with us for a while."

"I'm sorry to hear they're having problems and under normal conditions I'd be happy to have her come, but I'm not sure right now's the best time. Especially with everything that's going on around here."

"We'll be fine. Besides, I already told her she could."

"Brenda!"

"I'm sorry, but I just couldn't say no."

"So when is she coming?"

"Tomorrow."

Brenda could tell Brian was not very happy about Julie coming when there was a murderer still on the loose.

"Please don't be upset. Everything will be fine."

"I'm not upset. I just wish she wasn't coming right now. I don't want you putting your guard down because she's here."

"Stop worrying. We'll be fine."

"You'll take good care of us, won't you Shadow?" said Brenda, when Shadow started to whine from smelling the food she had taken out of the oven.

"Well I'm still going to have an officer keep an eye on the place until this is over."

"That's fine, but you better warn him that I'm packing heat now and I know how to use it," chuckled Brenda.

"I don't think that would be a good idea. I want him to show up, not scare the crap out of him!"

"Well if that's all it takes to scare a guy off, why don't you just put up a sign at the end of the driveway saying, DANGER! My Wife Has A Gun! BE AFRAID!"

"That might not be a bad idea," teased Brian.

"You're such a jerk!" said Brenda, grabbing the towel off the counter and swatting him with it.

Early the next morning, Brian was awakened when Brenda quickly got out of bed ~~and rushing~~ into the bathroom.

"Honey are you ok?" he asked.

Brian could hear Brenda gagging so he climbed out of bed and knocked on the bathroom door.

"Honey are you alright?" he asked again.

Brenda did not answer as he heard her gag again.

A minute passed before Brenda finally opened the door and came out. She looked pale as she walked over to the bed and sat down.

"Great, my sister's coming today and I'm sick!" said Brenda.

"Can I get you anything?"

Brenda shook her head no.

"I'm just going to lie back down for a little while and hope that whatever this is passes before she gets here."

Brian went into the bathroom and took a shower. When he came back out, Brenda was sound asleep.

After feeding the horses, Brian returned to the house to find Brenda still in bed, sleeping soundly. Quietly closing the bedroom door, he went back to the kitchen to fix himself a cup of coffee and wait for Jason to arrive.

Shadow was lying in the yard, under his favorite tree, when he spotted a patrol car coming up the driveway.

Brian knew Shadow had his eye on the car and stood there watching as Steve started to get out of his car. Shadow quickly jumped up and raced toward the car forcing Steve to leaped back inside as Shadow ran toward him barking. Brian went to the door and called for Shadow to come inside, but he continued to bark at Steve. Brian walked down to the car and sent Shadow to the house.

After talking with Steve, Brian headed back to the house. He was in shock as he wrote Brenda a note, grabbed his keys and hurried to his car.

Chapter 6

Brenda was still asleep when she was suddenly awakened by the ringing of the phone. Glancing at the clock, she was shocked to discover that she had slept until noon.

"Hello," she said sleepily.

"Hey Sis, I should be at your house around five thirty," said Julie.

"Ok good. I'm looking forward to seeing you."

"You don't sound very good. Are you ok?"

"I'm fine. My stomach has just been a little upset."

"I'm sorry, I hope you get to feeling better."

"I'm sure I will. I can't wait to see you."

"I'm looking forward to seeing you too. I'll be there soon."

"Ok, I'll be watching for you."

Brenda climbed out of bed and jumped into the shower. She walked into the kitchen and looked around for Brian when she spotted the note that Brian had left her.

His note said:

Sorry I left without saying goodbye, but I didn't want to wake you. Something came up at work and I had to go in. I called your work and told them you weren't feeling well and that you wouldn't be in today. I'll call you later. Love you, Brian.

Brenda made herself some coffee and as the aroma filled the kitchen, her stomach turned and she had to rush to the bathroom.

By three o'clock Brenda was finally feeling better and hurried to get the guest room ready for her sister.

As she searched the freezer for something to fix for dinner, the phone rang.

It was Brian.

"How are you feeling?" he asked.

"I'm feeling a lot better. Thanks for calling Regions for me this morning. I can't believe I slept until noon."

"Is your sister there yet?"

"No. She called to say she would be here around five thirty."

"Brenda I have something I need to tell you."

Brenda could hear the seriousness in Brian's voice.

"What is it Brian?"

"There's been another murder."

"Oh no, not again! Isn't this ever going to end?"

"Brenda, there's something else I think you should know."

Brenda suddenly had a sinking feeling in her stomach.

"What?" she asked, afraid to hear the answer.

"The girl that was murdered last night,.... was the girl Jason was out with."

Brenda's heart started to pound. She could hardly speak as she tried to comprehend what Brian had just told her.

"You can't possibly think Jason had anything to do with this!"

"I don't know what to think, but I do know before I go accusing him of anything, we have a lot of work to do."

"Well have you talked to him?"

"Honey I have to go. I just wanted to let you know what was going on and to tell you that I'll be working late."

"Brian!" said Brenda, wanting an answer.

"We'll talk later when I get home. I should know more then. I really have to go honey. Tell your sister I said hi and I'll see you both later."

Brenda was still in shock when her sister arrived. She hadn't been able to think about anything else ever since Brian had called her. She couldn't believe that Jason was at the police station being questioned about the murder. She felt sick again as she thought about Brian having to interrogate him.

Brenda sat at the kitchen table trying to take it all in when her sister arrived.

"I was beginning to think I'd never get here," Julie told Brenda as she walked up the steps of the porch to greet her sister.

"Well I'm really glad you're here."

"Are you ok? You look a little pale," said Julie, concerned for her sister's health.

"I'm fine. I just have a lot on my mind right now. Come on in and let's get you settled, then we can catch up on everything that's been going on."

As Julie unpacked, she told Brenda that she had found out that Mike, her husband, was having an affair with one of her best friends.

"Here I believed Liz was one of my best friends and then I find out she was a much better friend to my husband than to me!" said Julie.

"I'm so sorry. I never dreamed that Mike was the type of guy that would cheat on you!"

"Why didn't you tell me the two of you were having problems?"

"I really didn't think we were. Everything seemed fine. Mike's business has been doing really well. We rarely ever had a fight. I really didn't have a clue he was cheating on me."

"How'd you find out?" asked Brenda.

"He called me from work and said he had to stay late to talk to a new client. I really didn't think too much about it because he had been staying late a couple of nights a week for several months now. I guess that should have been my first clue, but anyway, after he called I decided instead of cooking, I'd go into town and get something to eat. I just happened to stop at one of those little strip malls on my way home," said Julie, pausing to take a deep breath, "and that's when I saw them."

"They were holding hands and laughing and smiling at each other as they went into the restaurant there."

"I can't imagine how you must have felt."

"What'd you do?" asked Brenda.

"First I just wanted to crawl back to my car and go home, but then my hurt turned to anger and I decided to go into the restaurant and confront them. I wanted them to know they were busted and couldn't lie their way out of it."

"OMG Julie! So what happened when they saw you?"

"Liz saw me first, and I think she about peed herself. Mike's back was turned to me so he didn't see me come in. Liz's guilty face said everything. She stared at me while she said something to Mike and then she rushed off to the bathroom. When Mike turned around and saw me standing there, he looked like he'd just been caught with his hands in his pants. I walked over to him and said. I can't believe it! You and Liz? Really Mike!"

"So what'd he say?"

"Nothing. He sat there speechless and wouldn't even look at me!"

"I told him I hated him and that he was nothing but a cheater and a liar and that I couldn't stand to look at him. Then I said if he knew what was good for him he better not come home. That's when he said he was So Sorry and that he still loved me."

"What about Liz? Did she ever come out of the bathroom?"

"No, because after I blew up at Mike, I marched into the bathroom and as soon as Liz started to open her mouth, I unloaded on her. I told her what a sorry excuse of a friend she turned out to be and that I never expected her, of all people, to go sneaking around behind my back with my husband or her husband's back! Then I told her that if she didn't tell her husband what she and Mike had been up to, I would!"

Brenda could see the pain and hurt in her sister's eyes as Julie said, "As far as I'm concerned she's just as bad as Mike and they deserved each other!"

Brenda gave Julie a hug and said, "I'm so sorry Julie."

"I wish I knew what to say to make you feel better, but I'm afraid I'm as shocked as you are."

"I'm just thankful you let me come and stay here with you and Brian while I figure out what I'm going to do."

"Well I hope you know you're always welcome and you can stay as long as you like."

"Thanks. You don't know how much that means to me."

"Have you told Mom and Dad yet?"

"No not yet, but I will. I'm just not ready to listen to any of mother's lectures right now. You know how she feels about Mike."

"Yeah, she thinks Mike can do no wrong. She's really in for a surprise!"

"I don't want to say anything to them until I've had a chance to get my head together. Then I'll spring it on them."

"Well be prepared, because you know mom's going to flip out when you tell her."

Brian sat in the interrogation room across from Jason.

"Do you want to tell me what happened last night?" asked Brian.

"If you're asking if I killed Carol, the answer's no. Of all people, I would think you'd know I'd never kill anyone," said Jason.

"It doesn't matter what I think, you were the last person to see Miss Dryer alive!"

Jason looked worried as he sat there staring at Brian as if none of this could possibly be happening.

"Listen Jason, if you want me to help you, then you'll have to tell me everything that happened last night."

Jason looked at Brian and after a moment he said, "I left your place and went home to shower. When I got out of the shower, I noticed that Carol had sent me a text message saying she wouldn't be able to leave work for another hour because her replacement was running late. She asked if I would mind picking her up at work instead of at her house."

"You say she worked at the Steak Barn?" asked Brian.

"Yeah. When I got there, she was ready to go. We decided to catch a show and after the show we went to Darby's for a bite to eat."

"What time was it when you got to Darby's?" asked Brian.

"I'm not sure. I picked her up around eight and the show lasted about two hours. So it must have been around ten or a little after."

"How long were you at Darby's?"

"Probably about an hour or so. Not long, because the band they had was playing so loud it was hard to talk, so we decided to leave right after we finished eating."

"Where'd you go after you left there?"

"I drove her back to her car. We sat there talking for about twenty minutes and then she said she had to

go because she had to get up early in the morning."
"We made plans to go out again on Friday and said
goodnight."
"Do you know about what time it was when she got
out of your truck?"
"Yeah, it was eleven twenty. The only reason I know
that is because she asked me what time it was just
before she said me she had to go."
"Did she happen to mention why she had to get up
early?"
"Yeah, she said she was starting a new job in the
morning and had to be there at eight.
"Did she say why she was changing jobs?"
"No, and I didn't ask."
Jason looked at Brian and Brian could tell he was
nervous.
Jason was thinking about the last time he was
arrested. He knew because he had a record, that he
was going to be Brian's number one suspect.
"Are you going to arrest me?" asked Jason, knowing
it wasn't looking good for him.
"We got a warrant to search your car and your
house, so it'll depend on what the officers find."
"You have to believe me Brian I had nothing to do
with this! I admit I screwed up before when I
pushed my stepmother and she fell and hit her head.
But as I told you, she was a drunk and when I saw
what she had done to my little brother because she

was mad at me, I lost it. I admit, I wanted to kill her, but I didn't and I certainly didn't kill Carol! Why would I?"

"I understand why you did what you did back then Jason, not that I think it was right. I just hope you understand that I've got a job to do and it's my job to check everything out."

"I understand that, but I'm telling you I didn't do anything to Carol, so you're not going to find anything."

"Then you have nothing to worry about."

"Tell me, did you happen to notice anyone hanging around outside when you dropped Carol off at her car?"

"No, but then I wasn't really looking for anyone either. I just dropped her off and waited until she got in her car and then I left."

"Did you see her drive away?"

"Not really, but I do remember looking in my rearview mirror and seeing her headlights come on as I pulled out."

"Brian, what possible reason would I have for killing Carol?"

"I don't know. People kill for a lot of different reasons. If there's anything I've learned from being a detective, it's that some killers don't seem to need a reason!"

Steve opened the door just then and motioned to

Brian.

Brian stepped out of the room and told Steve he didn't believe Jason killed Carol.

"Well maybe you better think again. We found these when we were searching Jason's house."

Steve handed Brian a bracelet that looked like the one Sharon Riker's mother had described and said her daughter was wearing when she reported her missing. Like Carol, Brian remembered that Sharon had also worked at The Steak Barn.

"We found this too," said Steve holding up a necklace.

"Where'd you find them?"

"They were hidden in this sock, in the back of his dresser drawer."

"I tried to warn you about him! Maybe next time you'll listen to me."

Brian felt sick as he stood there holding the jewelry that Steve had found. He didn't want to believe that Jason was the cold-blooded killer they had been searching for, because that would mean he had put Brenda in danger and it scared him to think about what could have happened to her.

All this raced through his mind as he headed back into the interrogation room.

"Are you sure you've told me everything?!" Brian asked Jason as he leaned across the table and stared into Jason's face.

"Yes... Why? What's going on Brian?" Jason asked nervously, wondering what had happened in the few minutes that Brian was gone.

"Would you like to tell me where you got this bracelet?" asked Brian, laying the bracelet on the table in front of Jason.

Jason looked puzzled as he stared at the bracelet.

"What's this about?"

"This was found hidden in your dresser."

"That's impossible. I've never seen that bracelet before in my life!" Jason's heart was pounding as he nervously stared at the bracelet.

"What about this?" asked Brian, laying the necklace on the table next to the bracelet.

"Have you ever seen this necklace before?"

Jason looking scared and Brian could tell he recognized the necklace.

"Answer me Jason. Have you ever seen this necklace before?" repeated Brian.

Jason continued to stare at the necklace and then he looked at Brian.

"It looks like the necklace Carol was wearing."

"I swear Brian, I have no idea how those things got in my house!"

Panic began to set in as Jason saw the disbelief written on Brian's face.

"Do you own a gun?" asked Brian.

"You know I do, but I didn't shoot anyone if that's

what you're really asking!"

"Who said Carol was shot?"

Jason looked confused.

"No one. I just assumed she was shot, since all the other women were shot."

"So where's your gun now?"

"I don't know."

"You don't know where your gun is?"

"No. I loaned it to my cousin a couple of months ago."

"What's your cousin's name?"

"Danny Hammill, but he doesn't have it either."

Brian looked at Jason now with skepticism on his face.

"I asked him to bring it back about a month ago and he told me he had misplaced it," explained Jason.

Brian sat there for a moment thinking and then he asked, "Has he been over to your place recently?"

"Yeah, he stayed over last night."

"Does he stay with you often?"

"Only if he's been out drinking."

"So he can verify what time you got home last night."

Jason shook his head. "No. He didn't come in until about two thirty in the morning."

Jason could tell by the look on Brian's face what he was thinking.

"You're thinking he might have murdered these women and planted that stuff at my house aren't you?"

"I'm not thinking anything yet, but I do need to question him and find out what happened to your gun."

"Where can I find Danny?"

"He works at Barney's out on Starkey Boulevard in Hartford."

Brian turned off the tape recorder and said, "I have to tell you Jason, it's not looking very good for you. If you can think of anything else, you need to let me know."

Jason looked worried as he looked at Brian.

"You're going to be taken down to booking and if you have a lawyer, it wouldn't hurt to call him. You should be able to post bond but I wouldn't leave town if I were you," said Brian, "

Brian walked out of the room and then Steve walked in.

"Well well, what have you gotten yourself into now?" Jason shot Steve a dirty look.

"Come on Romeo , you know the procedure."

"I want to call my lawyer," said Jason.

"I'm sure you do," smirked Steve, as he led Jason down to booking, "but not until we've taken your mug shot and fingerprints, but then you know all about that, don't you? After all, this isn't your first rodeo."

Brian drove out to Hartford to talk to Jason's cousin. Danny was working at the counter when Brian walked in and asked to speak to him.

"What can I help you with detective?" asked Danny.

"I understand your Jason Sloan's cousin."

"Yeah, so?"

"Did Jason loan you a gun?"

"Is this about me losing his gun?"

"I told Jason, I'd get him another one!"

"Did you?"

"Did I what?"

"Did you get him another gun?"

"No, why? And what's it to you if I did or I didn't?"

"Did you report the gun missing?"

"No, why would I? It's not like it was stolen!"

"How do you know that?"

"I just know! Hey what is this anyway?"

"When was the last time you saw Jason?"

"A couple of days ago!"

"What's this all about?"

"What kind of a gun was it that Jason had?" asked Brian.

"I don't know a hand gun. Something like the one you have."

"Am I in some kind of trouble?"

"You're sure it's been a couple of days since you were at Jason's?"

"No, I said it's been a couple of days since I've seen

Jason. I crashed at his place last night."

"You spent the night but you never saw him?"

"That's right. He was in bed when I got there and when I got up he was already gone."

"Well if you didn't see him last night, how do you know he was there?"

"Because his truck was parked out front."

"Where were you last night between eleven thirty and one?"

"Out. You know, having a couple of drinks."

"Where at?"

"Darby's, why? That's not a crime is it?"

"Did you see Jason there?"

"Yeah, he came in with this really hot brunette."

"Is this the girl he was with?" asked Brian, showing Danny a picture of Carol Dryer.

"Yeah, that's her."

"So how long were you at Darby's before you left?"

"I don't know! A while!"

"One hour, two hours?"

"I'm done answering your questions, unless you want to tell me what this is about!"

"There was another murder last night, and the girl who was murdered, was Carol Dryer."

Danny looked at Carol's picture again but didn't say a word.

"Have you ever seen this girl before?" Brian, was holding up a picture of Sharon Riker now.

"I don't know. I see lots of girls."

"Look again!"

Danny looked at the picture again and said, "Maybe, maybe not. Like I said, I see a lot of girls."

"So you're not sure?"

"No, and I have to tell you, I'm getting really tired of all these questions. So, if you don't mind, I'd like to get back to work."

Brian placed a card on the counter and said, "Here's my card. If you happen to think of anything else, call me and if you happen to find that missing gun, I suggest you let me know."

Brian drove away feeling that he now had three suspects. Jason, the mystery guy at the bar, and Danny Hammill.

Brian stopped at Darby's on his way home and picked up their surveillance tapes. No one at Darby's remembered what time Danny Hammill had left, so Brian hoped that these tapes would give him the information he was looking for.

Brian called the police station and asked Max to go to The Steak Barn to see if they had surveillance cameras set up in their parking lot. He wanted everything he could possibly get on the nights Sharon and Carol were murdered.

Shadow jumped up and ran to the door when he heard Brian's car pull up to the garage.

"Brian must be home," Brenda told Julie.

The girls came out of the guest room when they heard Brian come into the house.

"Hi Brian," said Julie, giving Brian a hug. "Thanks for letting me stay here."

"You're welcome," said Brian.

"Hi Honey," said Brenda, giving Brian a hug and a kiss. "You look exhausted."

"Why wasn't the door locked?" Brian asked Brenda.

"It wasn't?"

"No it wasn't!"

"I must have forgotten to lock it when Julie got here."

"Brenda, you need to be more careful!"

"I know, I'm sorry."

"So tell me, what's been going on with the serial killings I've been hearing about?" Julie asked Brian.

Brenda and Brian looked at each other and Brian could see Brenda's concern for Jason.

"Brenda probably told you there was another murder last night."

"No she didn't. There was another murder?"

"Do you remember me telling you that Brian hired a friend of his to help us out around here?" Brenda asked Julie.

"Sure, I remember. His name was Jason, wasn't it? And I think you said he was on Brian's polo team."

"Well the girl Jason had a date with last night, is the girl they found murdered early this morning."

"And you think he's the serial killer?" Julie asked Brian.

"All we know right now is that he was the last person to see her alive and he doesn't have an alibi for the time she was murdered."

"Well there's no way Jason would hurt anyone, let alone kill them!" Brenda said.

"Well I thought the same thing, until some jewelry belonging to two of the dead women was found in one of his dresser drawers!"

Brenda looked shocked, as she stared at Brian.

"Are you saying you think Jason's the serial killer?" she asked.

"I'm saying, it's not looking very good for him right now."

"Well have you talked to him about it?" Brenda asked anxiously.

"Yes darling, I talked to him this morning when he was brought in for questioning."

"What'd he say?"

"He denied having anything to do with it and he said he had no idea how the jewelry got in his house!"

"I just can't believe this is happening," said Brenda.

"How were the girls killed?" asked Julie.

"Like the rest of the women. Their wrists and ankles were bound with duct tape. They were both stripped naked and shot at point blank range in the head. Carol, the girl Jason was with, had bruises on her arms and legs, but there weren't any signs of her being sexually molested."

"Were there any signs of blood in Jason's vehicle?"

"No blood and no gun was found in his truck, or at his house."

"So the only real evidence you have is the jewelry that was found at his house?"

"That, and no way to substantiate his alibi."

"Don't you find it odd that of all the women who've been murdered, only two pieces of jewelry were found? Usually if a serial killer's going to collect souvenirs from his victims, he'll take something from each of them," said Julie

"Good point," said Brian.

"Do you have any other suspects?" asked Julie.

"Two," said Brian, "but right now I don't have much to go on. Jason's cousin really doesn't have an alibi for either of those nights and he did have access to Jason's house and a gun. We're still looking for the other guy. The only problem with him is, he didn't have access to Jason's house."

"Does Jason have a lawyer?" asked Brenda.

"I don't know, why?"

"Brenda... whatever you're thinking you can forget it," said Julie.

"But you are an attorney and Jason could use a good

attorney right now."

"Hold on sis!" said Julie.

"I'm just saying..."

"Brenda. Do you had any idea how long this case could drag out? I wasn't planning on staying here forever!"

"Would you girls mind if we drop this so I can get something to eat?" asked Brian.

"That's a good idea," said Julie. "I'm getting pretty hungry myself."

When dinner was finished, Brian told Brenda he had to go back to the station to pick up some things. "I shouldn't be too long," he said.

"Ok," said Brenda. "Are you going to talk to Jason again?"

"He should have bonded out by now so if you're thinking I should talk to him about your sister, I got the impression she really didn't want to defend him."

Brenda had a defeated look on her face as Brian gave her a kiss and said goodbye.

"Brian?"

"Yeah honey."

"I just want you to know I love you and no matter what happens and I know you'll find the person responsible for killing those women."

"Thanks honey. I'll see you girls later."

Brian gave Brenda another kiss and as he was

leaving, he locked the door on his way out.

"What a mess," Brenda said to Julie. "I still can't believe this is happening. The whole thing seems like a terrible nightmare."

"Listen sweetie, I know you're worried, but you need to have some faith in your husband. He'll get this figured out."

"I know. It's just that Jason doesn't deserve this. If he was a killer, wouldn't I have noticed him acting strangely?"

"Possibly, but look at all the people who live right next to killers. They go around believing they're the nicest people too, until they're convicted of murder."

"Ok, you've made your point," said Brenda.

When Brian arrived at the station he called a meeting with all the officers working the case.

"I want everything you can get me on Carol Dryer," Brian told the officers.

"Her friends, anyone she's dated and if the same man that was hitting on Sharon Riker was at The Steak Barn the night Miss Foley was killed."

"I also want you to find out everything you can on Jason's cousin, Danny Hammill."

Brian asked Max, "Did you get those surveillance tapes for me?"

"Yes I did. There on your desk," he said.

"I also questioned everyone that was working that

night, but no one remembered anything unusual."
One of the other officers said, "Jason only has one
gun registered in his name and it's the same caliber
as the one the serial killer's been using. The
problem is, we still haven't been able to locate it."
"Well in Jason's defense, he never tried to hide the
fact that he had a gun," said Brian. "But he did say
he had loaned it to Danny Hammill and Hammill
admitted that Jason had loaned him his gun, so it's
really important that we find that gun."
"Do you want me to get a search warrant for his
place?"asked Max.
"Yeah, and get one for his place of work too.
According to him he lost it. Hammill also had access
to Jason's house so that makes him a suspect,
especially since there were no fingerprints found on
the jewelry."
"We really need to find that gun guys, so keep
looking," said Brian.
"Any luck finding that Jerry guy yet?" asked Brian.
"Not yet," said Max, "but we're getting closer. We
did find out that his last name is Snyder. We're
watching his place now and there's an APB out on
him. It's only a matter of time before we get him."
As the meeting ended, Brian said, "I don't want
anyone screwing this investigation up. I want every
I dotted and T crossed. Is that understood?"
"Good! Then let's get back to work!" said Brian.

Brian stood there looking at the evidence board as everyone except Steve left the room.

"Tell me you still don't believe Jason's innocent after what we found at his house!" said Steve.

"I don't know what to think. I just find it hard to believe he's this cold blooded serial killer."

"All I know is before I go charging him with murder I don't want any doubts about his guilt or innocence. Right now we still have two other suspects to consider, so I have no intention of leaving any stones unturned in this investigation!"

"Well personally, I think he did it and you better be careful, with him running loose he may just decide to go after Brenda."

"Well if you're so convinced he's guilty, shouldn't you be out there trying to locate that gun instead of standing here talking to me?"

Steve was surprised by Brian's attitude as he watched him gather up the surveillance tapes that lay on his desk as he prepared to leave for the night.

"You look beat," said Steve. "Why don't you let me take those tapes and go over them for you?"

"No thanks, I'd rather do it myself. I'll see you in the morning."

Brian was exhausted when he finally crawled into bed that night, but as tired as he was, his mind continued to race as he laid there, refusing to let him sleep. Jason had been released and told not to leave town, but Brian continued to have mixed feelings regarding Jason's innocents or guilt. He looked over at Brenda who was sound asleep next to him. I have to continue protecting her, he told himself. Until this case is solved and the killer is locked away, I'm going to have to have an officer keep an eye on her and her sister for me.

Unable to sleep, Brian quietly slipped out of bed, went into the den, and picked up one of the surveillance tapes.

"Alright, let's see if there's anything on here that can help me," he said to himself.

As he put the tape in he heard someone behind him. He turned and saw Julie standing there.

"I couldn't sleep either," she said.

"What are you doing?"

"I thought I'd look over these surveillance tapes. I'm trying to figure out if that Jerry Snyder guy or Jason's cousin, were at The Steak Barn on the night Sharon Riker or Carol Dryer were murdered."

"Mind if I join you?"

"No, have a seat."

Julie sat down next to Brian as he started the tape from the night Carol Dryer was murdered.

Less than half way through the tape Brian noticed Carol speaking to a couple of her co-workers before going over to the table where the man, now known as Jerry Snyder, was sitting.

Carol had spoken briefly to Jerry before taking his order and as she walked away, Jerry kept his eye on her. When she finally returned with his order, Brian and Julie both commented that she seemed uncomfortable while he was talking to her. This continued to happen each time she went back to his table.

Shortly after that, Brian noticed Carol heading for the front door and noticed Jason waiting there for her. They greeted one another and then left together.

"So far everything fits the story Jason told me," Brian told Julie.

"I didn't notice anyone other than that Jerry guy keeping an eye on Carol," said Julie.

"No, I didn't either. Let's take a look at the tape from the parking area. Hopefully it'll show someone other than Jason in the parking lot when he dropped Carol off at her car."

Brian and Julie watched carefully as Jason's truck pulled up next to Carol's car. Again, Jason's story matched what he had told Brian. They sat in the truck for a short time talking and then Carol got out and they watched as she got into her car and drove off in the opposite direction from Jason. As the tape continued, Brian carefully watched for anything suspicious after they had left the parking lot.

"Did you notice that?" asked Brian, quickly backing

up the tape.

"What," asked Julie?

"Some headlights came on and a car pulled away in the same direction as Carol's, shortly after she drove away."

"I didn't notice anyone coming out of the restaurant while they were in the parking lot," stated Julie.

They watched again as Carol drove off and seconds later, another car pulled out of the lot, just as Brian had said.

"You're right. That is strange," said Julie.

"That Jerry guy left the restaurant after they did," said Brian. "But I don't remember seeing his car leaving the parking lot on the tape. Did you notice him driving away?"

"Not that I recall, but how would he know Jason would be bringing Carol back to the restaurant to get her car? I find it hard to believe he'd just hang out there," said Julie.

"Unless he was waiting for one of the other waitresses to get off work," said Brian.

"Or," said Julie. "He may have noticed Carol's car still in the parking lot and came back later to see if it was still there."

As the tape continued, Julie said, "Is there any way to get a better look at the car that left after Carol did?"

"Not here, but I'm sure it can be done by our computer expert when I get to work tomorrow."

"What's on these other tapes?" asked Julie.

"They're from the night the Riker girl was killed."

"I started looking at them after her murder, but kept getting interrupted. I had one of my other detectives take a look at them for me, but he said he didn't see anything that would help."

"Who didn't see anything?" asked Brenda.

"What are you doing up?" asked Julie.

"I'm sorry babe, did we wake you?" asked Brian.

"No, I had to go to the bathroom and noticed the light was on."

"So what are you two up to?" asked Brenda.

"We're going over these surveillance tapes," said Brian.

"Mind if I join you?"

"Of course not," said Julie, sliding over on the couch to make room for Brenda.

As the three of them sat there studying another tape from the Steak Barn, Brian suddenly paused it.

"What is it?" asked Brenda.

"That's Jason's cousin. Danny Hammill and he's talking to the Riker girl."

"So what's unusual about that?" asked Brenda.

"It wouldn't be, except he told me he didn't know her."

Brian started the tape again and they watched as Danny continually called Miss Riker over to his table.

"She's smiling," said Julie, "but look at her body language," said Julie.

"She looks stiff and irritated," said Brenda.

They watched Danny leave his table and walk up to the bar. Minutes later, another man walked up to the bar and stood next to Danny.

"That's Steve!" said Brenda. "Did he tell you he was out there that night?"

"Who's Steve?" asked Julie.

"No, he never mentioned it," said Brian, confused as he watched Steve standing there talking to Danny.

"Who's Steve?" Julie asked again.

"Steve's one of the detectives that works with Brian," Brenda explained.

"He wouldn't happen to be the detective you asked to look at these tapes for you was he?" Julie asked Brian.

"Something's not adding up," said Brian.

Brian was wondering why Steve hadn't mentioned he was at the Steak Barn the night the Riker woman was killed, and why he never mentioned talking to Danny.

"Why wouldn't he tell you he spoke to Jason's cousin?" asked Julie.

"I don't know, unless it's because Danny wasn't a suspect at that time, or maybe he didn't know Danny was Jason's cousin. Hell, I didn't even know Jason had a cousin until Carol Dryer was murdered."

"But why wouldn't he mention it to you later? When he found out that Danny was Jason's cousin and Danny was named as a suspect?" asked Brenda.

"I don't know, but you can bet I'll be asking him that first thing in the morning."

Confused, Brian started the tape up again.

They watched as Danny got up and left right after speaking to Steve.

"Danny doesn't seem very happy," said Julie. "Look at the way he's carrying himself. It's as if he's angry about something."

"Steve has that effect on people!" said Brenda.

Brian rolled the tape back and watched again as Danny walked up to the bar, and until he left.

"You're right," said Brian. "He does act like Steve said something that he didn't like."

They continued to watch as Steve got up from the bar and moved to an area that was out of the camera's range. About a half hour later, they noticed him leaving and a short time after that, Jerry Snyder came walking into the bar. He took a table in Sharon Riker's area and just as the owner had told him, Carol waited on him that night.

"He's not looking to happy about having Carol as his waitress instead of Sharon," said Brenda.

"No he doesn't," replied Brian.

"Look at how he's watching Sharon and Carol," said Julie.

"He definitely doesn't seem very happy," said Brenda.

They watched as Jerry walked up to Sharon and took a hold of her arm. They had words as she pulled her arm free and then she disappeared into the kitchen.

"He looks angry. It's too bad we couldn't hear what they were saying," said Brenda.

They continued to watch and shortly after Jerry's confrontation with Sharon, he paid his bill and left. Brian put in the tape that showed the parking area from that night, but it only showed Jerry speeding off and later Miss Riker and Carol coming out together and getting into their cars and driving away.

"That was the last tape," said Brian.

"I think we should get to bed," said Julie, yawning as she stretched her arms, "or none of us will get any rest tonight,"

They each looked at one another and Brenda said, "Right! Like we're going to be able to fall asleep now!"

"Well we should at least try," said Brian, as he stood up and held his hand out to Brenda.

Brenda took his hand and they all headed off to bed.

Chapter 7

 Brenda woke up to the smell of coffee. When she walked out into the kitchen, she found Julie sitting at the kitchen table, eating an English muffin and sipping on a cup of coffee. The smell of the coffee made Brenda feel nauseous and she had to turn around and rush to the bathroom.

When she finally returned to the kitchen Julie asked, "Are you still feeling sick?"

"I felt fine until I smelled that coffee!"

"You're not pregnant are you?" Julie asked jokingly.

"Hardly."

"When was the last time you had your period?"

"I don't know, maybe five or six weeks ago, but you know that I never have regular periods."

"Well don't you think you ought to go to a doctor to be sure?"

"I'm not pregnant!"

"Really! Well how long have you been having morning sickness?"

"Morning sickness? I don't have morning sickness!"

"It's probably just some kind of flu bug."

Julie gave Brenda one of her looks and asked again, "How many days Brenda?"

"Three, counting today," admitted Brenda.

"Don't you think if it was the flu you'd be over it by now?"

Brenda rolled her eyes.

"I really think you should call your doctor and get checked."

"That's all I'd need right now with everything else that's been going on."

"If I had to tell Brian I was going to have a baby, on top of everything else he's dealing with right now, that would really push him over the edge!"

"Well maybe you'll find out it is just a flu bug. You have been using protection haven't you?"

Brenda remembered back to the night she and Brian had sex after they got home from the Steak Barn.

And then there was the night they had make-up sex.

"There were a couple of times we didn't ..."

Julie smiled. "Call the doctor and make an appointment."

"Alright already! Can I at least eat some breakfast first?"

"Sure, sit down and I'll fix you some bacon and eggs."

Within a few minutes, Julie sat a plate of food down in front of Brenda. She took one look at the food and rushed off to the bathroom.

A smile crossed Julie's face. "Right. You're not pregnant."

Brian was at the station looking over the shoulder of their computer expert. They were looking at the surveillance tape that had the suspicious car in it.

"Is there any way we can get a better view of that car?" Brian asked.

"I'm afraid this is the best I can do," the expert said, after clicking some buttons.

"You can't get it in any clearer than that?"

"Let's see," he said as he tapped a few more keys on his computer.

"Sorry. I'm afraid that's it."

"It looks like it could be a police car," the expert said.

"Yeah, I just wish we could tell for sure."

"Ok, thanks," said Brian, as he stared at the car on the screen.

Brian collected the tapes and took them back to the evidence room.

"I want you to notify me if anyone asks for these tapes," Brian told the officer in charge of evidence.

"You got it," he said.

As Brian walked back to his office he passed Steve in the hallway.

"I need to see you in my office," he said.

"Ok," said Steve, as he turned and followed Brian back to his office.

"What's up?"

Brian took a long hard look at Steve and then asked, "Why didn't you tell me you were at the Steak Barn

the night Miss Riker was killed?"
Steve looked surprised and on edge by Brian's question.
"I don't know. I guess I didn't think it was important. It's not like I noticed anything suspicious."
"Maybe it wouldn't seem important to mention to a normal person, but you're a cop and I can't figure out why you wouldn't mention it to me. Especially since you spoke to Danny Hammill that night."
Brian could tell Steve was nervous and growing angry as he continued questioning him.
"How do you know Danny Hammill?"
"I don't!"
"Then what were you talking to him about?"
"I just noticed he was hitting on the Riker girl and went over to tell him he was wasting his time, that's all."
"How do you know he was wasting his time?"
"Because she didn't act like she was interested in him and he didn't look like her type."
"If that's all there was to it, then why wouldn't you come and tell me about it?"
"Like I said, I didn't think it was important!"
"You didn't think one of our suspects hitting on a young woman the same night she was murdered was important?"
"What are you trying to say Brian? You're not

accusing me of having something to do with these murders are you?!"

"I don't know, did you?"

"Listen, I know Jason's your friend, but you're not going to pin this on me!"

"You just can't accept the fact that Jason killed those women can you?"

Steve looked angry as he growled, "So this is what I get after all these years of being your partner? You're going to accuse me of being a murderer! Thanks, thanks a lot!" he spat.

Steve stormed out of Brian's office nearly running over Captain Phillips as he came down the hall.

"What was that all about?" the Captain asked Brian.

"I think we should talk," Brian told the Captain.

Brenda had called her doctor and made an appointment for three o'clock.

It was now two forty-five and she and Julie were just getting into the car to head for his office when Jason pulled in.

"Who's that?" asked Julie.

"It's Jason," said Brenda, as she got back out of the car.

"Brenda, be careful," said Julie, concerned for her sister's safety.

Brenda walked over to Jason as he climbed out of his truck. He had backed up to his horse trailer and looked at Brenda as she approached his truck.

"I'm just here to pick up my horse," he told her as he got out of the truck.

"Jason, I'm so sorry about all this. I want you to know I don't believe for one minute that you killed that girl or anyone else."

Jason looked into Brenda's dark, worried eyes and knew she meant what she was saying. He suddenly realized what a good friend she really was. His heart sank as he looked at her sad face. He knew their friendship had to come to an end and it tore at his heart. His biggest regret was that he'd never be able to tell her how he really felt about her.

"Thanks for your vote of confidence, it really means a lot to me, but I'm afraid you're the only one who feels that way."

"That's not true. I'm sure Brian feels the same way I do and I know he's trying his best to prove you're innocent!"

"I'm sorry, but I really don't want to talk about this right now."

"Weren't you getting ready to leave?"

Brenda looked over at Julie who was watching them. "Yes, but..."

"Then I think you should go."

Brenda stood there for a moment as Jason turned away and walked to the back of his truck. She turned and started walking toward the car when she heard Jason say, "Shit!"

"What's wrong?" asked Brenda.

"I forgot to change the ball on my hitch."

"Well why don't you just take the one off Brian's truck? I know he wouldn't mind if you borrow it."

"Are you sure?"

"Of course I'm sure. I'll tell him I said you could take it."

"I'll get it back to him as soon as I can."

"No problem. We won't be using the trailer for awhile anyway."

"Thanks Brenda."

"Take care Jason and keep your chin up. I'm sure things will work out." Brenda forced a smile but her heart was breaking as she looked into Jason's drawn, tired looking face.

"Is everything alright?" asked Julie as she noticed the sad look on Brenda's face.

"No. No it's not! I wish this awful mess was over with and they had the real killer in jail so that everything could go back to normal!"

When Brenda walked from the doctor's office into the waiting room, she looked numb.

"Well, what'd he say?" Julie asked anxiously.

"He said I'm pregnant," said Brenda, still not believing what he had told her was true.

"Oh honey, that's wonderful!" Julie said totally excited.

"When are you due?"

"Sometime around the middle of March."

"Oh my gosh! This is so exciting! I'm going to be an Aunt!"

They walked out to the car and Brenda slid into the front seat feeling numb.

"Auntie Julie. It has a nice ring to it, don't you think?" Julie asked cheerfully.

"Yeah, nice."

"What's wrong? Aren't you happy? You're going to be a mommy!"

"I just don't know if I'm ready for this! I've never really been around little kids. What if I'm a terrible mother?"

"Will you stop. You're going to be a great mother and I know Brian will be a wonderful father."

Brenda started to tear up and Julie said, "Oh sweetie, don't cry. Everything's going to be fine."

Tears rolled down Brenda's cheeks as Julie tried her best to reassure her.

"Come on sis, smile. You'll see, everything's going to work out."

"I'm sorry, I just feel like an emotional wreck right now," Brenda said as tears ran down her cheeks.

"That's just because your hormones are all screwed up. Wait until mom finds out! Then you'll really have something to cry about!"

"Oh god, mom!" said Brenda.

Julie started laughing. "Let's get you home. We're going to have to start planning on where you want to put the nursery, and Mom's room."

Brenda had a look of horror on her face as they looked at one another and Julie couldn't help but laugh.

Captain Phillips had left Brian's office and was sitting at his desk deep in thought. Was it possible that one of his detectives had something to do with the murders of these women? Brian really had no solid evidence to back up his suspicions. Just a video that looked like it could be a patrol car seemingly following one of the women that was murdered, and what seemed like a cover up of information. He had to admit that Brian had made some good points. Steve did have access to Jason's house and the opportunity to plant evidence. He didn't have an alibi for the time of the murders and he had withheld the fact that he had been at the Steak Barn. Brian felt that Steve should be watched, at least for the time being, while he finished his investigation. Captain Phillips didn't want to think about the field day the press would have if it did turn out that one of his officers was the serial killer.

Brian left the police station still feeling troubled over his conversation with Captain Phillips about Steve. Saying his suspicions out loud made it seem all the more probable that Jason wasn't the killer and that he needed to take a hard look at Steve, Danny and Jerry.

As Brian drove through town, he noticed Max's car parked at Darby's and pulled in. He knew he could trust Max and he needed someone he knew he could talk to.

When Brian walked in he spotted Max sitting in a corner booth and went over to join him.

"Hey Max, mind if I join you?"

"No, have a seat."

"Is something going on?" asked Max.

"I just need someone I can trust to bounce some things off of."

"Sure, fire away."

Brian began by telling Max that he was beginning to think that Steve may have something to do with the murders.

"Steve never mentioned that he was here the night Carol was murdered and he never mentioned that he had talked to Danny that night."

"But what about the jewelry that was found at Jason's house?"

"Steve or Danny could have easily planted that jewelry at Jason's. They both had access to his place and if Jason was the killer and was collecting objects from the women he killed as souvenirs, why were there only two pieces of jewelry found at his place?"

"So are you saying you think Steve or Danny is trying to frame Jason for those murders?"

"I know it sounds crazy, but Steve's car was parked along the road by my place when I went home for lunch and he was no where around."

"Did you ask him about it?"

"Yeah, he said he stopped along the road to take a pee!"

"And you don't believe that."

"It just seems awfully strange that his car would be parked out there at a time when I normally wouldn't be around, and that right after that the Riker woman was murdered, those pictures of Brenda and Jason just happened to appear at the murder scene."

"You think Steve planted those pictures there? Why would he do that?"

"I'm not sure but he's never liked Brenda and he was pretty upset when he found out I had hired Jason to work at my place. He kept telling me that I couldn't trust Jason or Brenda."

"Even if it wasn't Steve who took those pictures and it was the murderer, then Jason couldn't be the killer!" said Brian.

Max had to agree that things just weren't adding up.

"Then there's Danny," said Brian.

"He admitted to me that Jason had loaned him his gun and that he hadn't returned it. So what happened to it?"

"But how would Steve have gotten a hold of Jason's gun?"

"That I haven't figured out yet, but then we still don't have any proof that it was Jason's gun that killed those women either."

"True," said Max.

"Have you talked to the Captain about all this?"

"Yeah, I just finished talking to him before I stopped here."

"What'd he say?"

"Just that we should keep a close eye on Steve. He doesn't want to believe that one of his officers could have anything to do with this and neither do I, but...."

Max looked concerned as he waited to hear the rest of what Brian had to say.

"There's one more thing."

"What's that?"

"On the surveillance tape, the night Carol Dryer was murdered... it looked like one of our patrol cars followed her out of the parking lot after Jason dropped her off."

"And you think it might have been Steve's?"

"It's just a hunch, but I'm beginning to think there's a good chance that it could have been."

"Wow, I had no idea!"

Max sat there quietly thinking about everything Brian had told him.

"You don't think that's how Steve got his hands on all those women do you?" asked Max.

"What do you mean?"

"You hear about it all the time. A cop pulls over some unsuspecting girl for a bogus traffic stop. Tells her to get into his patrol car while he calls her license in, and bang, he has her."

Brian hadn't thought of that, but he felt Max made a good point. It would be an easy way for a cop to get access to women.

"You're right. Even if a car went by and saw them stopped along the road, they wouldn't think anything of it."

"I'm not saying that's what happened," said Max.

"I know, but it is a possibility."

"So what do you want me to do?" asked Max.

"I'd like you to keep an eye on Steve for me and if he goes anywhere near my place I want to know about it."

"Will do," said Max.

As soon as Brian pulled into his driveway that evening he noticed that Jason's horse trailer was gone. He hurried to the house to check on the girls and when he opened the door, he could hear Julie's laughter coming from the den. Shadow raced over to greet him, as both women followed him into the kitchen. Julie had a big smile on her face as she greeted Brian, while Brenda looked a little pale and was acting nervous as she walked over and gave him a kiss.

"What have you two been up to today?" Brian asked, looking from one to the other.

"Not much," Brenda quickly replied.

"I see Jason's trailer is gone."

"He was here to pick up Star," said Brenda.

"Did you talk to him?"

"We were just leaving when he pulled in, so yes, I talked to him."

Brenda looked into Brian's eyes but couldn't tell what he was thinking.

"I still don't believe he had anything to do with killing anyone!" said Brenda.

"Well until I know that for sure, I still want you to be cautious. As a matter of fact, I want both of you to be cautious of anyone who shows up here."

"Would you like something to drink?" Julie asked Brian, giving him a big smile.

"No, I'm fine," said Brian, wondering why Julie was smiling at him like a schoolgirl with a secret, and feeling as if something was going on that he didn't know about.

"Is everything ok? You two are acting a little strange."

"Everything's fine," said Brenda, as she gave her sister a look that said, stop smiling at him like that!

"You're sure everything's ok?" he asked, looking at Julie and then at Brenda.

"I told you, everything's fine," said Brenda.

"Ok, well I'm going to go jump in the shower."

"That's a good idea. Dinner will be ready shortly."

As soon as Brian had left the room Brenda said, "Would you stop grinning at him like that? He's a detective, remember? He gets suspicious about everything!"

"Then you better get in there and tell him the news!" Brenda looked nervously at the door to their bedroom.

"I think I should wait until after dinner. You know, until I see what kind of a mood he's in."

"Brenda, Brian's always in a good mood! You're just stalling,"

"I am not stalling, I'll tell him after dinner."

"Ok, but I'm going to hold you to that."

After they had all finished eating Julie said, "Would anyone care for desert?"

"Sure, I'd love some," said Brian.

"Julie baked an apple pie, especially for you," Brenda told Brian.

"That was thoughtful of you Julie. Thank you."

"Well it's kind of a special occasion," said Julie.

"Really? What occasion is that?"

Brenda's eyes were wide as she glared at her sister.

"Julie just means I went to the doctor today," Brenda blurted out.

"Doctor? Are you ok?" asked Brian. His voice full of concern.

"Yes darling, I'm fine."

Brian looked at Julie nervously. "Then why do I have a feeling you're not telling me something?"

Brenda nervously glanced at Julie and then back to Brian.

"The doctor said I was suffering from morning sickness. I'm pregnant."

Brian sat there for a moment in shock, as Julie and Brenda looked at each other and waited for his reaction to the news.

"Did you hear me? We're going to have a baby."

"You're going to have a baby?"

"Are you sure?"

"Yes, I'm pretty sure. That's why I've been sick every morning for the last few days."

"How? When?"

"Well I would hope you know how!"

"Yes, I know how! But when? When's the baby due?"

"Sometime around the middle of March."

"I'm going to be a father!" laughed Brian, as he snatched Brenda up into his arms and gave her a big hug.

"We're going to have a baby," he said to Julie, smiling from ear to ear.

"Yes I know and I'm going to be an Aunt!" Julie said, her voice filled with joy and excitement.

"Congratulations. I couldn't be happier for the two of you."

Brenda started to feel a little better as all the excitement lifted her spirits.

The next morning Brenda was suddenly awakened when she heard Shadow barking excitedly from the kitchen. She quickly sat up and then suddenly felt sick to her stomach as she got out of bed and hurried into the bathroom.

When she finally came out of the bathroom, she could hear voices coming from the kitchen. Slipping on her robe she walked out of the bedroom toward the kitchen. She could see Brian sitting at the table with a cup of coffee and trying to read the newspaper while Julie talked excitedly about the baby.

As Brenda entered the kitchen both Brian and Julie were beaming as they looked at her.

"Good morning darling. How are you feeling?" asked Brian.

"Well I just puked, but I think I'll live."

"What have you two been talking about, or need I even ask?"

"Nothing much," said Julie with a big smile.

"Right! That's why I heard something about how excited mom's going to be when she finds out she's going to be a grandmother?"

Julie smiled, "Oops. Don't worry I won't say a word. I plan on giving you the pleasure of telling her the good news."

"I just can't help thinking about how much fun it's going to be to shop for baby things."

Brenda walked up behind Brian, slid her arms around his neck, and gave him a kiss on the cheek. "What are we going to do with her?" Brenda asked Brian. "She's already been after me about setting up a nursery."

"Well it wouldn't hurt to start thinking about where you'd like to put it," said Brian.

Brenda rolled her eyes and said, "You know, you two need to settle down! It's not like I'm going to have this baby any time soon. So if you two wouldn't mind, I'd like to at least try and eat something, before you rush me off to the hospital."

Brian smiled at Julie who was grinning, and then he said, "I guess I better go out and feed the animals before I get into trouble."

"I'll go with you," said Brenda, wanting to get away

from any conversations with Julie about shopping for baby things.

Brenda didn't want to admit to herself or anyone else, that the thought of having a baby frightened her.

"I thought you wanted something to eat!" said Julie.

"I'll eat when I come in."

"Well then I'll come with you. What about you Shadow, would you like to come too?"

Shadow barked and danced around the kitchen excitedly. Brenda looked at Brian with dismay on her face before heading to the bedroom to change her clothes.

Brenda walked into Hank's stall with some feed and he nudged her affectionately as she stroked his neck.

"Do you think the doctor will let me ride while I'm pregnant?"

Brian looked at Julie and she shook her head no.

"Do you really think that would be a good idea? You know how Hank likes to buck when you get on him."

"I know, but he's just playing and he doesn't buck that hard, do you big guy?"

"I guess that's something you'll have to discuss with the doctor."

Brenda picked up a brush and started brushing Hank while Julie stood outside his stall watching. Brian had gone into the hay mound to throw down a few bales of hay and Julie decided to join him.

"Can I help?" she asked Brian.

"If you want," said Brian. "Grab a couple of those bales of straw over there and throw them down this chute."

"I don't get it," Julie said to Brian.

"I thought Brenda would be a lot more excited about having a baby then she is."

"Give it time. I'm sure it hasn't quite sunk in yet. I know I'm still trying to digest the thought of being a father."

"I guess. I just know if it were me, I'd be looking at pictures of nurseries in magazines and picking out paint colors and furniture as soon as I found out I was expecting."

Brian smiled, "Well you have to remember, the only thing this pregnancy has done for Brenda so far, is make her sick!"

Julie laughed. She loved Brian's sense of humor and she was happy that her sister had found such a great guy. Suddenly Julie felt sad as she thought about her five years of marriage. She hadn't been able to conceive and now her husband was having an affair. She had to wonder if that was the reason he had sought out someone else. Tears welled up in her eyes as she threw the last bale of straw down the chute.

Brian looked at Julie and noticed her sudden mood change and the tears in her eyes.

"Are you ok?" he asked.

"Yeah, I'm fine," she said, but Brian could hear the sadness in her voice.

No one said a word as they walked back to the house. Brenda had noticed the change in Julie's mood too and thought it was because of her lack of excitement over being pregnant.

"How about if we all go into town tomorrow and have breakfast. Then afterwards we could start looking around for some furniture for the nursery," said Brenda, trying to sound cheerful to lighten the mood.

"What do you say Dad? Can you spare a couple of hours from work to go look at baby furniture with us?"

Brian quickly glanced at Julie and saw the light come back into her eyes.

"I think I could manage that."

Brenda let out a little sigh and said, "It's all settled then."

"Look out world Auntie Julie is taking the Nichols baby shopping."

Julie was all smiles now and Brenda was glad that the mood had suddenly changed back to a happier one.

By the time they had returned home from shopping, Brian and Brenda were exhausted.

They had been shopping for hours and Brian would have sworn they had looked at everything you could possibly buy for a baby.

Brian was in agony as he looked at all the boxes and bags in the back of his truck. All he could think about was how expensive everything was and all the work that lay in front of him putting it all together.

"Honey, why don't you and Julie go inside and rest while I unload all this. You look exhausted and I can get this," said Brian.

"I'm fine," said Brenda. "I can help you bring some of

this stuff in."

"Brenda, do what Brian said. I'll help him with this. You need to get off your feet and rest," said Julie.

"I'm not an invalid. I'm just pregnant."

Brian gave Brenda a look that said, just humor us and do what I asked.

"If you want to help, why don't you go inside and fix us something to drink? I could really use one about now."

"That sounds good. I could use one too," said Julie.

"Alright you two, I'll go but don't even think about setting any of this up tonight. I still need to paint before we put anything in the nursery."

"Don't worry," said Brian, "I don't feel like putting anything together right now anyway."

"Now will you go and unlock the door so we can get all this stuff inside?"

"Alright already! Man you're getting bossy all of a sudden!"

Brenda unlocked the door of the house, but instead of fixing drinks, she headed into the room that would soon become their nursery. Looking around, she thought about all the work that still needed to be done before the room was ready for furniture.

Her thoughts were interrupted when she heard Julie complaining about how heavy the box was that they were trying to get through the door and Brian was telling her to be careful not to pinch her fingers.

Chapter 8

A month had passed and there were no new breaks in the case. Although no more bodies had been found, Brian had a feeling it was just a matter of time before the killer would claim his next victim.

As Brian sat at his desk looking at the rap sheet on Jerry Snyder, Officer Slone stuck his head inside Brian's office and said, "We finally busted that Snyder guy. They're bringing him in now for questioning."

"Thanks Max. Let me know as soon as they arrive."

Brian looked through the observation window into the interrogation room at Jerry Snyder. He sat slumped over in his chair with his hands folded in front of him and his head down.

"Want me to go in there with you, while you question him?" asked Steve.

"Not this time," said Brian.

"How's come?"

"Because I want to talk to him alone."

Jerry looked at Brian when he threw a folder down on the table in front of him. Then Brian took a seat and looked him straight in the eye.

"You have quite a rap sheet Jerry."

"Yeah, so what!" he said sarcastically!

"Do you know this girl?" Brian asked, as he took a picture of Sharon Riker out of the folder and shoved it toward Snyder.

Snyder glanced at the picture and said, "Yeah, I've seen her around."

"Did you know she was murdered?"

"Is that why you dragged me down here? You think I killed her?"

"Didn't you?"

"No. Why would I?"

"I understand you've been hanging around the Steak Barn where she works."

"Well the last I knew there's no crime in that!"

"Maybe not, but it must have made you mad when you asked her out and she kept turning you down."

Snyder looked angry as he stared at Brian, but he didn't say a word.

"I know I'd be upset if I asked a girl out after she had been flirting with me and always went out of her way to wait on me and then she blew me off for no reason."

Brian could tell he had touched on a sore spot.

"It had to make you angry, especially when she asked someone else to wait on you so she wouldn't have to talk to you."

Snyder continued to glare at Brian.

"Did you know she was shot in the head? That the

killer took all of her clothes off, raped her and then bound her hands and feet before he shot her."

Snyder had a smug look on his face now when he said, "No I didn't, but I'm not surprised."

"You're not surprised because you think she deserved to die? Because you were so angry at her for embarrassing you, you decided to teach her a lesson by raping and shooting her?"

"I'm not surprised because she was a tease," said Snyder.

"Have you ever seen this girl before?" asked Brian as he pulled a picture of Carol Dryer out of the folder and slid it across the table.

"Yeah, she works at The Steak Barn," said Snyder.

"Did you know that she was murdered last night?"

"Anyone who listens to the news would know that."

"I know what you think Detective. You think that because I have a rap sheet I must be your serial killer. Well I hate to disappoint you Detective, but I had nothing to do with killing those women. So unless you have some kind of proof, I'm out of here!"

"Not yet you're not!" said Brian. "I still have some questions I need answered."

"You can't keep me here. I know my rights!"

"Where'd you go after you left the restaurant on the nights Sharon Riker and Carol Dryer were killed?"

"I went home and went to bed."

"Did anyone see you when you got home?"

"No."

Brian gave Snyder a long hard look, picked up the folder and the pictures from the table and walked out of the room.

"I want him held until our guys have finished searching his place and car," said Brian.

Sgt. Slone nodded toward the door. "Here they are now."

Brian walked over to the officers and asked, "Did you find anything?"

"We found these pictures of Sharon tacked up on his bedroom wall, but that was about it."

"What about a gun?"

"We didn't find a hand gun, but we did find a sawed-off shot gun."

"Ok, book him on a weapons violation. What about his car?"

"Forensics has it."

"Ok, I'm going to head down there."

Brian wasn't surprised that a handgun wasn't found. Snyder had more than enough time to ditch it when he was on the run but he was surprised when nothing turned up in his car.

Something wasn't adding up about these murders that kept bothering Brian. All of the murders had the same MO but one. But yet, there were three different guns used. All the women killed before

Sharon Riker's murder, were shot with the same 40-caliber handgun. Sharon however, had been shot with a 38-caliber, and the markings on the 40-caliber bullet that killed Carol Dryer didn't match the others. So did the serial killer use more than one gun to try and throw them off? Or is Jerry Snyder Sharon's killer and there's more than one killer still out there?

Could Danny Hammill have used Jason's gun and then lost it somehow, forcing him to use a different gun to kill Carol? Or is Jason the killer and Danny's covering for him?

Then there's Steve. Is he the killer and the one that's been spying on Brenda, hoping to catch her alone so he can kill her? Brian thought again about Steve's car being parked near his house and the lame excuse he had given for being out there.

Jerry Snyder had the motive for killing Sharon, and he did disappear right after Carol Dryer was murdered, but did he kill those other women? Brian started to get a headache as all of these unanswered questions ran through his head.

Brenda and Julie had finally decided on the color of the paint for the nursery. Julie had suggested a sunny yellow while Brenda preferred a sky blue, so they compromised and picked out a light celery green color that they both liked.

"Do you want to go to town tomorrow and pick up the paint and some paint supplies?" asked Julie.

"I guess we could," said Brenda.

Julie had the impression that Brenda wasn't at all enthused about the idea of painting.

"I'm sorry if I seem pushy. I just want to help you get some of this done while I'm still here."

"I know, and I appreciate the fact that you want to help. I guess I'm just feeling a little overwhelmed with everything right now."

"We don't have to go tomorrow. It was just a thought."

"No you're right. I've been wanting to get that room painted anyway, so I guess tomorrow would be as good a time as any to get started on it."

"What time do you thing Brian will be home?" asked Julie.

"It's hard to say. He usually calls me around this time to let me know if he'll be here for dinner."

"Speak of the devil," said Brenda, as the phone began to ring.

"Hi Honey, we were just talking about you."

"Were you now? I hope it was something good."

"Well I had nothing but good things to say about you, whereas Julie had some pretty horrible things to say."

"That's a lie!" yelled Julie.

Brian smiled and said, "I should be home in about an hour. Do you lovely ladies feel up to going out tonight instead of cooking?"

"What do you think?" said Brenda.

"I'll take it that's a yes, so I'll see you shortly."

"Ok, we'll be here."

Brenda hung up and said to Julie, "We have a date tonight with my handsome husband, so we better get the horses fed and get ready."

The girls decided to go off their diets for one night and told Brian they wanted to go out for pizza. As they ate, Brenda asked Brian if there was anything new on the murder case.

"Jerry Snyder was picked up and brought in this morning, but unfortunately we weren't able to find a hand gun."

"Do you think he did it?" asked Julie.

"It's hard to say. None of our suspects have solid alibis, and right now I don't have anyone other than Snyder that had a motive."

"So do you think he killed the Riker girl because she refused to go out with him?" asked Brenda

"Possibly. It's hard to say and he's not talking."

"But what reason would he have had for killing Carol or all those other women?" asked Brenda.

"It's hard to imagine what justification a killer uses

for murdering someone," suggested Julie.

"Well unless that gun turns up, everything's just speculation right now," said Brian.

"You haven't turned him loose have you?" asked Brenda.

"No, he's being held on a parole violation right now."

"What about Steve's gun? Have you sent his gun down to the ballistics department to be checked out?" asked Julie.

"No. I spoke to Captain Phillips and he wants me to hold off on that for right now. We really don't have anything on him except my suspicions and he's the only one who had an alibi for the night Carol was murdered."

"You mean because he was working on patrol that night," said Brenda.

"Right, but here's the other problem I'm dealing with. We have two different ballistics reports. Either the killer used two different guns or there's more than one killer running loose out there."

"Good lord," said Julie. "I don't know how you do it Brian! Talk about a stressful job!"

"Maybe we should change the subject," said Brenda.

"That's a great idea! Want to talk about the baby?" asked Julie, smiling at Brenda.

"No!" Brenda said with a stern face.

Brian and Julie both looked at Brenda and were surprised that she was so adamant on the subject.

"Ok then...want to talk about the weather?" Julie asked.

Brian smiled and slid his hand down the length of Brenda's thigh, giving her leg an affectionate little squeeze just above the knee.

"Sorry," said Brenda, realizing how that must have sounded.

 "I think my hormones must be raging."

 It was a quiet ride home that night, as everyone seemed to be lost in their own thoughts.

When they arrived at the ranch, Brian held the door open for the girls as they went inside.

Mentally exhausted Brian went into the den and sat down. Brenda came in shortly after him and told him that their neighbor, Mr. Morgan, had called and left him a message.

 "He wants you to give him a call. He says it's important."

"He probably wants to renew his lease on the field."

"Well don't forget to call him back."

"I'll call him first thing in the morning. Right now all I want to do is have my wife sit down next to me and relax."

Brenda smiled and snuggled up against him. He slid his arm around her and ran his hand over her belly.

Brenda smiled and put her hand over his.

"I love you babe."

"I love you too," said Brenda, kissing him tenderly. "Are you still going to love me when I'm all fat and swollen and have to stand two feet away from the stove to reach it?"

"Two feet! You're not going to get that big are you?" teased Brian.

"Maybe…Why?"

"You do realize my stomach's going to blow up like a balloon don't you?"

"I'm just teasing you honey. You really need to lighten up or our baby's going to think her mommy doesn't want her."

"Her? What makes you think I'm going to have a girl?"

"Her, him, I don't know, it could be a boy."

"Would you rather have a girl?"

"It really doesn't matter. I just want it to be healthy. I'll love it no matter what sex it is."

"Don't you want a boy?"

"I never said I didn't want a boy!"

"Well I think a boy would be nice, especially if he's anything like his daddy."

"Maybe you'll have twins. A boy and a girl. That would be nice."

"Please, don't wish that on me! Could you imagine having to buy double of everything?"

"Well your sister would love it!" chuckled Brian.

Brenda smiled and rested her head on Brian's

shoulder.

"We're really going to have a baby aren't we?"

"I sure hope so, after all the baby furniture we just bought!"

"We really did go a little overboard didn't we?"

"Yeah... I don't think we should go shopping for baby stuff with your sister anymore."

"I know. She was like a person on crack looking for her next fix."

Brian and Brenda started laughing and Brenda suddenly felt better. Maybe being a mother won't be so bad after all, she thought.

"You're going to be a wonderful father," said Brenda.

"And you're going to be a great mother."

Brenda smiled at Brian as he pulled her close and kissed her.

Julie was up early and was busy making breakfast when Brian got up and came into the kitchen.

"The coffee's all ready," she told him as he walked over to the window and looked out at the barn.

"Have you always been an early riser?" he asked Julie.

"Pretty much. Mornings have always been my favorite time of the day. Is my sister up yet?"

"Not yet. She's not feeling very well again this morning."

"I'm making pancakes. Would you like me to fix

yours now, or do you want to wait for Brenda."

"I can wait. I'll go down to the barn and take care of the horses and maybe Brenda will be up by the time I get back."

A short time later Brenda wandered into the kitchen wearing her robe and looking tired and pale.

"Brian said you weren't feeling very well this morning."

"No I'm afraid not. This morning sickness is kicking my butt. Has Brian left for work already?"

"No, he's feeding the horses."

"I know we talked about going into town this morning to get paint for the nursery, but I'm really not feeling up to it right now."

"That's fine. We don't have to get it today."

Brian had caught part of their conversation as he came through the door and asked, "Where are you two going?"

"We were going to go into town to get some paint for the nursery," said Brenda, "but I'm afraid it's going to have to wait until I'm feeling better."

"Do you have to go into work today?"

"I was planning on it. Did you need me to stay here and help you do something? I have to warn you though, I'm not much of a painter."

Brenda shook her head no and then she said, "I'm going to go lay down for a while."

She gave Brian a kiss and then headed back to bed. "How long does this morning sickness last?" Brian asked Julie.

"It's hard to say. Sometimes it only lasts a couple of weeks and sometimes months. I've even heard it can last throughout the whole pregnancy."

Brian looked at Julie with surprise and despair on his face.

"God I hope not!" he said.

Julie laughed.

"Me too, but it'll all be worth it in the end," she said.

By noon Brenda was up and feeling better, so she and Julie decided to give Brian a call to see if he could meet them at Darby's for lunch.

"I wish I could honey, but there's been another murder."

"Oh no." said Brenda.

"What?" asked Julie.

"There's been another murder," Brenda told Julie. "I'm afraid I'll probably be late getting home, so don't hold dinner for me."

"Ok. Oh Brian? Did you have a chance to call Mr. Morgan this morning?"

"No, I didn't. Would you mind calling him for me? I'm pretty sure it's about renewing his lease."

"Ok, I'll give him a call as soon as we get back home."

"Thanks babe. I've got to go. You girls have fun, but be careful."

"We will."

When Brenda hung up the phone Julie said, "Well if nothing else, at least this murder eliminated one suspect."

"What do you mean?"

"Well unless this murder took place before he was arrested, Jerry Snyder can't be the killer!"

After lunch, the girls returned home with their paint and painting supplies and decided to start on the baby's room. By six o'clock, they had it finished and both girls were exhausted.

"It looks great doesn't it?" asked Julie, as she admired their work.

"I have to admit, it really does look pretty darn good for two rookies!"

"Wait until we hang the curtains and get the furniture set up in here."

"I'm really glad we changed our minds and decided to go with this color."

"I am too. It'll be fine for a girl or a boy, don't you think?" Julie asked Brenda.

"I think so," said Brenda.

"I can't believe you don't want to know what sex your baby's going to be. Doesn't Brian want to know?"

"We talked about that last night and we both decided we'd rather wait until the baby is born to find out."

"Why don't you go in the kitchen and find something for us to eat while I start cleaning up this mess," said Julie.

"I really should go out and bring the horses in and get them fed before I do anything else."

"You know Brian doesn't want you going out to the barn alone," warned Julie.

"Yes I know, so I guess you'll just have to come with me. That way I can tell Brian I wasn't alone!"

Brenda and Julie were getting ready to walk out when Brenda suddenly stopped, "I almost forgot. I was supposed to call Mr. Morgan back."

"Well you better call him before we go to the barn or you'll probably forget again."

Brenda picked up the phone and rang Mr. Morgan's number.

"Hello?"

"Hello Mr. Morgan, this is Brenda Nichols. You called and left a message for Brian?"

"Oh, yes. Hello Brenda. Never mind dear, it's all ready been taken care of."

Brenda was puzzled. "What's been taken care of Mr. Morgan? Did Brian call you?"

"No, he didn't call me."

"Then I'm afraid I don't understand."

"You see I was combining the corn in the field next to your place when I found a gun laying in one of the corn rows. I was going to give it to Brian, but then I saw an officer parked over by your place and told him about it. He asked me where I found it, so I took him to the field and showed him. He took it with him and I told him to make sure he told Brian about it. He did tell him didn't he?"

"I really don't know, but I'll be sure to ask Brian about it."

"Mr. Morgan you wouldn't happen to remember what the officer's name was that you gave the gun to would you?"

"Let me think....I believe his name was Officer Wade."

"Does that sound right?"

Brenda's heart started to pound.

"Yes, thanks Mr. Morgan."

"Tell Brian I need to talk to him about renewing my lease on his field."

"I will and I'll make sure to have him call you."

"Ok Brenda. It's been nice talking to you."

"You too Mr. Morgan."

Julie noticed the strange look on Brenda's face as she hung up the phone.

"Is everything ok?" she asked.

Brenda shook her head.

"What is it?"

"Just a minute. I need to call Brian."

Brenda picked up the phone and dialed Brian's number.

"Detective Slone."

"Hi Max. Is Brian there?" Brenda asked with urgency in her voice.

"No, I think he just stepped out of his office for a minute. Is everything ok?"

"Can you have him call me as soon as he comes back? It's important that I talk to him."

"Sure. Is it something I can help you with?"

"I just need to know if Steve told him about the gun our neighbor found in his cornfield, so please have him call me as soon as he can."

"I'll be sure to give him your message."

"Thanks Max."

Brenda hung up the phone and Julie asked again, "What's going on Brenda?"

"Let's go feed the horses and I'll fill you in on the way to the barn," said Brenda.

As they left the house, Brenda said, "I think I know who the serial killer is," said Brenda. Her eyes were large and dark as she looked at Julie.

"Who?"

"I think it could be Steve."

"Steve? The detective who works with Brian?"

Brenda's heart was pounding as she told Julie what

Mr. Morgan had said about finding the gun.

"I'm sure Brian would have told me about Mr. Morgan finding a gun and handing it over to Steve if he knew about it. That's not something Brian would keep from me, so I'm certain Steve never told him about the gun!"

"Maybe he did and it turned out to be nothing, and that's why Brian never mentioned it to you," suggested Julie.

"I don't think so. I think it was Steve in the cornfield the day Shadow ran off. He may have grabbed Steve and Steve hit him trying to get free and dropped the gun.

"Well I'm sure Brian will figure it out when you tell him what Mr. Morgan said."

"You need to relax and stop worrying about this. It isn't good for you or the baby to be stressed out all the time. Brian will handle it."

As they entered the pasture the horses lifted their heads and started walking toward them. Julie said, "I'll take Brian's horse. I don't feel like getting a hunk bitten out of my arm by that crazy horse of yours!"

"Hank wouldn't hurt you. It's men he doesn't like not women."

"Because he's psycho!"

"No, because he was abused by his owner!"

"Who just happened to be a man?"

"That's right and that's why he doesn't trust men."

"Nice try, but I'm still going to keep my distance from him."

 After the horses were taken to the barn and fed, the girls were heading back to the house when they saw a truck pull in.

Shadow started barking and Brenda grabbed his collar.

"Who's that?" asked Julie.

"It looks like Jason's truck," said Brenda.

"What's he doing here?"

"He borrowed Brian's hitch the other day so he's probably returning it."

Jason turned off his truck and climbed out.

"Hi Brenda," he said, as he reached into the bed of his truck.

"Hey Jason," Brenda said with a smile.

Just then, a patrol car came racing down the driveway and stopped.

"What's going on?" Julie asked Brenda.

"I'm not sure."

Julie and Brenda watched as Steve jumped out of his car and pulled his gun from his holster.

Brenda and Julie stood there in shock when Steve pointed his gun at Jason.

Chapter 9

Brian called Max and asked him if he had located Jason, Danny or Steve.

"I need to know where they were last night between 11:00 pm and 12:30 am," Brian told him.

"If any of their alibis don't check out, I want them brought in for questioning."

"I'm on it," said Max.

"Oh and Brian, I forgot to tell you Brenda called."

"Ok, thanks. Did she say what it was about?"

"No. Just that she wanted you to give her a call."

Brian tried calling, but was interrupted. He decided the call would have to wait until he returned from the captain's office.

"Drop your weapon and put your hands behind your head!" Steve yelled at Jason.

"What's happening?" Julie asked Brenda nervously.

"I don't know," said Brenda.

"What the hell Steve? I don't have a weapon! I'm just here to return the ball from Brian's horse trailer."

"What's going on Steve?" Brenda asked, as Shadow growled and pulled at his collar.

Jason had started to hold up the ball for Steve to see, when suddenly Brenda and Julie heard two shot's ring out.

"Oh my god, oh my god!" Brenda gasped as she watched Jason fall to the ground.

Startled and panic stricken, Brenda ran to Jason's side. He was lying face down on the ground and he wasn't moving.

"Call 911!" yelled Brenda, in a state of panic as she felt for Jason's pulse.

Everything seemed to explode after that, as Brenda watched what seemed like a horror movie being played out in her own back yard.

Shadow raced toward Steve the minute Brenda let go of his collar and leaped into the air, grabbing Steve's arm. Steve dropped his gun as Shadow clamped down with his teeth and began shaking his head. Steve fought to free himself from Shadow's jaws when another police car came racing down the driveway.

Max jumped out and pulled his weapon as he rushed toward Steve.

Brenda screamed, "Shadow! Leave it!"

And Shadow released Steve's arm and ran back to where she and Julie were kneeling beside Jason's body.

"He's dead!" cried Brenda.

"Steve shot Jason for no reason!" she cried out to Max.

"Put your hands on top of your head Steve and turn around," said Max.

Max picked up the gun that Steve had dropped and began patting Steve down. He discovered another gun, hidden in Steve's belt and as he pulled it out, Steve said in a desperate voice, "Max, you don't understand! That's Jason's gun. Jason's the serial killer! He was coming here to kill Brenda!"

Brenda was furious with Steve now, "Don't listen to him Max! He's crazy! Jason was just bringing Brian's hitch back! If anyone's the killer it's him!"

"Max you have to listen to me!" said Steve. "That's the gun we've been looking for. I had ballistics check it out. It's the same gun that was used to kill all of those other women and it's registered to Jason!"

"How'd you get this gun?" asked Max.

"Brian's neighbor gave it to me. He found it out in the cornfield and turned it over to me to give to Brian."

"So Brian knows you have it?"

"No, but only because I wanted to have it checked out to be sure it was the weapon used in the murders. When I found out it was Jason's gun, I started following him. That's how I knew he was coming here."

Brenda felt confused and frightened as she listening to Steve's explanation.

Not wanting to believe Steve's story, she asked, "If you're not the killer, then why'd you shoot him? He told you why he was here and he wasn't armed so how would he have killed us?"

"You have to believe me Brenda. He was coming here to kill you!"

"Well I don't believe you!" yelled Brenda. "If anyone was coming here to kill me it was you!"

"Brenda's right Steve. Jason wasn't coming here to kill her," said Max.

Steve stared at Max. "What about the gun? I had it checked out."

Steve saw something in Max's eyes that he had seen in other killers.

"You," said Steve. "You stole Jason's gun from his cousin...you're..."

Max had a blank look on his face as he pulled the trigger and shot Steve twice in the chest.

Brenda and Julie both jumped when they heard the gun go off and saw Steve drop to the ground.

Brian had returned to his office and tried again to call Brenda. Still unable to reach her, he then tried to contact Max to see if he had had any luck in locating his three suspects. When he was unable to reach Max, he tried again to call Brenda. When she still didn't answer, he had this strange feeling that something wasn't right.

"I need to run home for a while," Brian told one of his officers. "If you should hear from Max tell him to call me."

"Sure thing Brian," said the Officer.

As soon as Shadow heard Max's gun go off, he sensed Brenda and Julie's fear. Seeing Max as a threat, he immediately charged him. Brenda jumped to her feet and yelled, "Shadow no!" Terrified for his safety she yelled again, but he didn't stop.

Max quickly stepped back and fired his gun, hitting Shadow in the shoulder and sending him tumbling to the ground.

He laid there whimpering as Brenda raced to his side. Dropped to her knees, she lifted his head onto her lap and stroked his neck. Tears streamed down her face as she glared at Max.

"For god's sake Max, what the hell's gotten into you?" yelled Brenda!

Pointing the gun at Julie now, Max said, "Get up, both of you!"

Brenda slowly got to her feet as Julie walked over to her side. Realizing he was going to kill her and that now he'd have to kill Julie too, Brenda spat out angrily, "You're not going to get away with this!"

"Sure I am, and you want to know the best part? Steve's going to be blamed for it," he said in a calm, egotistical voice.

"You're insane if you think you'll get away with this!"

"You know what Brenda, Steve was right. You are a smart mouth little bitch! Now, both of you march your tight little asses up to the house," demanded Max.

Both Brenda and her sister were terrified as they walked toward the house. Max had them stop for one brief moment while he reached into his car and pull out a roll of silver duct tape and a paper bag.

Once inside the house he ordered Julie to take off all her clothes and put them in the bag.

"Don't do it Julie," said Brenda. "He's going to kill us whether we do what he says or not."

Max glared at Brenda and pointed the gun at her head.

"Take them off, or I'll shoot your sister right in that smart mouth of hers!" he told Julie.

Julie quickly began removing her clothing. When she had gotten down to her bra and panties, she stopped.

"All of them!" he shouted, as he took a step toward Brenda.

"Don't hurt her, please," cried Julie, as she quickly

slipped off her panties and bra and dropped them into the bag.

Julie stood there trembling. Naked and exposed, she tried to cover herself with her hands, while Max stood there blatantly staring at her naked body before ordering her to get down on the floor. Brenda could see Julie's whole body trembling, as she did what he asked.

Looking at Brenda now, Max tossed her the roll of silver tape.

"Wrap that around your sister's hands and feet!" he demanded.

Brenda stood there with the tape in her hand, praying for Brian to show up before it was too late.

He swung the gun in Julie's direction and said, "Would you rather I shoot her right now?"

Brenda pulled off a large piece of the tape and kneeled down next to Julie.

"I'm so sorry," she told her sister as she wrapped the tape around Julie's wrists.

"Now her feet!" demanded Max.

Brenda could see the fear and the tears in her sister's eyes as she wrapped the tape around her sister's ankles. Julie's lips began to tremble as she looked at Brenda and said, "It's all right. I love you sis."

"Now you!" Max told Brenda, as he pointed his gun at Julie. "Get your clothes off and put them in the bag with hers!"

As Brenda started to undress, she was trying to figure out how she could get to the bedroom and get her gun.

"Brian's going to kill you when he finds out what you've done!"

"I don't think so. Brian's a good detective, I'll give him that, but he'll never figure out it was me."

"What makes you think that?" Brenda asked, as she tried to stall for time.

"I told you. I plan on making Brian believe that Steve's our killer."

"Brian's not stupid. He won't just take your word for it."

"I think he will when I tell him Steve came here planning to kill you with Jason's gun to make it look like Jason did it. But when Jason showed up to return your husband's hitch, Steve had to kill him, to keep him quiet. I pulled in and saw Steve shoot Jason in cold blood causing Steve to panic and turn his gun on me. I had no choice, I had to shoot him."

Brenda stood there staring at Max in disbelief. He had concocted the perfect crime. She knew Brian was already suspicious of Steve and now she feared that Max actually could get away with this.

"Now, are you going to finish getting undressed or am I going to have to shoot your sister?"

Brenda slid her jeans off and as she put them in the

bag, she noticed Shadow's head peering around the kitchen door.

"You really think you're going to get away with this don't you?" asked Brenda, trying to distract Max. "I can just imagine how your poor wife is going to feel when you finally get caught and she discovers she's been living with a serial killer."

"Shut up!" yelled Max.

Brenda saw Shadow crouch low to the floor and leap, sending Max crashing to the floor. Brenda quickly looked for something to hit Max with so she could grab his gun, but he got to it first. Shadow sunk his teeth into the calf of Max's leg and he gave out a yell as he struggled to free himself from Shadow's jaws. Terrified Brenda ran for the bedroom to get her gun. A shot rang out and for an instant Brenda froze. She quickly reached for the drawer and pulled it open. As she fumbled through her clothes, Max grabbed her by the hair and yanked her backwards. Brenda fell to the floor and then spun herself around. Fighting for her life now she kicked Max as hard as she could in the crouch. He doubled over in pain and grabbed for her leg. Brenda quickly rolled out of his reach and scrambled to her feet. Grabbing the lamp off the nightstand, she hit him, sending him sprawling to the floor. He grabbed for her again, cursing as he watched her run from the bedroom.

Brenda was hoping that Max would follow her so she could lead him away from Julie and hopefully buy them some time. As she ran for the door she looked at her sister lying helpless on the floor and noticed Shadow's lifeless body lying in a pool of blood.

Once outside, adrenalin raced through Brenda's body as she ran for the barn. She felt as if she were going to throw up when she pasted Jason and Steve's bodies, lying in the grass, next to Jason's truck.

As Brenda reached for the barn door, she heard two shots ring out. She paused and looked back at the house. Brenda dreaded the worst when Max stepped out of the house and leaned against the doorway, as he searched the darkness for her.

Brian was speeding towards home when he received a call.

"We haven't been able to locate Steve or Jason yet and we can't seem to get a hold of Max either," said the officer on the other end of the line.

"Well keep trying to reach Max and let me know as soon as you do locate him!"

Brian tried calling his house again, but there was still no answer. For some reason tonight reminded him of the night Dr. Fowler had Brenda taken to

Silver Lake and left her there.

Brian's heart started to pound as he tried to call Julie's cell phone and got no answer. He had let it ring until it finally went to her voice mail. He left her a voice message saying, "Julie its Brian. Is everything all right? I've been trying to reach Brenda, but she's not answering the phone. Call me as soon as you get this. I'm on my way home now."

Brenda pushed the door to the barn open and ran inside. Hank nickered when he saw her and she quickly unlatched his stall door and pulled it closed behind her. Trembling, she crouched down in the corner, trying to make herself as small as possible. Hank lowered his head and touched her face with his nose. Suddenly he jerked his head up and looked out over his stall door.

"I know you're in here Brenda."

"You're only kidding yourself if you think you can hide from me."

Brenda, frozen in fear, sat huddled in the corner.

"I shot your sister Brenda. I wish you could have seen her face when I put the gun to her head and pulled the trigger."

Brenda was trembling uncontrollably now. Hatred filled her body and it was all she could do to keep from attacking him.

Knowing she'd be next, Brenda thought about the unborn child she was carrying, and knew that somehow, she had to get back to the house and get her gun.

Brenda was silent as she sat there hoping that Max would go up into the hay mound thinking she was up there. She knew her only chance was to sneak out of the barn and back to the house.

Max stood quietly in the isle, listening for any little sound. He looked around the barn and noticed the latch on one of the horse stalls wasn't fastened. "So that's where you are," he said.

He walked over to the stall and pushed the door open. Hanks ears went flat to his head and Brenda could see the hatred in his eyes as he charged Max. Max's gun flew from his hand as he crashed against the wall behind him. Hank bit down on Max's shoulder as he struggled to get to his feet and away from Hank's pounding hooves. Max tried desperately to get to his gun, but Hank stomped on his hand as he reached for it.

Hank had him pinned against the wall, biting at him, as his hooves struck Max's legs.

Brenda quickly got to her feet and made a mad dash for the barn door. Running as fast as she could, she headed straight for the house.

Hank kept Max pinned until he saw Brenda run from the barn. He bolted after her, following close behind her until she reached the house.

Once inside Brenda quickly locked the door and turned toward the bedroom. Her foot slipped as she hurried across the kitchen floor. Looking down, she stopped and dropped to her knees. She had slipped on the blood that was coming from her sister's head. Brenda reached down and pushing the hair away from Julies face. All the fear that Brenda had been feeling drained from her body as she walked into the bedroom. Anger and hatred had replaced her fear, as she reached into the drawer and took out her gun. Determined now to end this, she cocked the gun and released the safety.

Blocking out the horror that lay in front of her, she unlocked the front door. She remembered what Brian had told her. Make yourself as small of a target as you possibly can. So she lay on her stomach next to her sister, aimed the gun at the door, and waited.

Chapter 10

As Brian raced for home, he received a call from the station.

"Brian, we just had a 911 call from your neighbor."

Brian's heart started pounding. "What was the call?"

It was from a Mrs. Morgan. She said she thought she heard gunshots over at your place. We're sending a car out there now."

"I'm almost there. Send a rescue too. Just in case we need it."

"You got it Detective."

"And see if you can locate Max!"

Max limped back to the house, holding his arm. He was surprised to find the front door open as he climbed the porch steps.

He walked inside, and noticed Brenda lying on the floor next to her sister holding a gun. She seemed calm and her face was expressionless as she pointed her gun at him.

Max smirked. "Do you really think you can kill a person Brenda?"

Brenda didn't answer. She just stared at him with a blank look on her face.

Max smiled, "You're not going to shoot me."

"That would make you a killer just like me."

Max noticed Brenda's hands were beginning to shake.

Smiling he took a step forward and Brenda aimed her gun a little higher.

"Put the gun down Brenda. You don't have it in you to shoot," he said with confidence in his voice.

"You killed my sister," said Brenda.

"That was your fault. You shouldn't have run off."

Max slowly started to raise his gun. "That horse of yours injured my shooting arm, but luckily I'm still a pretty good shot with my left."

"You should have killed me when you had the chance," said Brenda.

There was a calmness about Brenda that Max hadn't expected and it was unsettling to him. He was used to women crying and pleading with him to spare their life.

Max stared into Brenda's eyes and lifted his gun.

Brian slammed his car into park and jumped out. As he looked around, his fears turned to panic when he saw Jason and Steve's bodies lying on the ground. "BRENDA?" he yelled. "Oh dear god no, please, not my wife."

Brian was racing for the house when he heard three shots ring out. His heart was in his throat as he pulled his gun and cautiously looked through the open door of the kitchen. The first thing Brian noticed was the blood spatter on the walls. Then he saw Shadow lying in a pool of blood a short distance from the door. Panicking, he cautiously stepped inside and looked around the kitchen. Max lay on the floor bleeding from two gunshot wounds to his chest. Julie lay naked on the floor with Brenda sitting next to her, struggling to free her hands from the tape. Julie's face was stained with blood and Brenda's gun lay on the floor next to her.

Brian slowly walked over to Brenda trying hard to stay calm. He could hear the rescue coming in the background as he slowly picked up the gun and set it on the counter.

Brenda looked at Brian with a blank, helpless look on her face. He could tell she was in shock as he spoke softly to her.

He picked her up and carried her into the bedroom, wrapping a blanket around her. Brian reached for another blanket as Brenda lay down and curled up into a ball.

Brian could hear all the activity that was taking place outside as the police and paramedics arrived. "Brenda, I'll be right back. I'm going to cover Julie up," said Brian.

Captain Phillips came walking through the door along with several other officers.

"What the hell happened out here?" he asked Brian,

as he looked around the room.

"I'm not sure," said Brian, as he covered Julie with the blanket.

Brian went back to the bedroom, lifted Brenda into his arms, and carried her from the house. She stared off into the distance and was unresponsive as Brian carried her over to the rescue truck.

After the paramedics had finished examining her, Brian climbed into the rescue and held her in his arms as more rescues arrived with stretchers. Brian watched as they carried Julie from the house and put her in one of the other rescue trucks.

"I'm so sorry Julie. I'm so sorry," whispered Brenda.

When Brenda arrived at the hospital, she was taken to a room in the ER. Brian told the ER physician that Brenda was pregnant and wanted to know if the baby was all right. The doctor ordered an ultrasound and then told Brian the baby was doing fine. Brenda had been given a mild sedative to help her relax and within minutes, she drifted off to sleep. Brian called Brenda's parents and told them the devastating news. They told Brian they would be on the first flight out and would call him as soon as they arrived.

Brian looked over at Brenda and took her hand as she lay sleeping peacefully. Tears filled his eyes as he thought about what could have happened to her and their baby. He was worried that all this stress would end up affecting her health and the baby's.

Around 5:00am, Brian had finally drifted off to sleep. He was suddenly awakened by the sound of footsteps. It was a friend of his, who happened to be one of the paramedic's who was called out to Brian's house.

"Hey Brian, I thought you should know that Max died on the way to the hospital. Apparently one of the bullets nicked his heart and he bled to death."

"Thanks, Sam."

"How's she doing?"

"She's hanging in there. The doctor gave her something to relax her."

"Did you get a chance to see her sister before they took her to surgery?

"What? Her sister's still alive?"

"I thought you knew. There doing emergency surgery on her right now."

Brenda suddenly cried out. She was having a nightmare and it was all Brian and Sam could do to keep her from pulling her IV out of her arm, as she thrashed around in the bed.

When she had settled down and was resting again, Brian said, "Thanks Sam. I'm glad you told me about Max and Julie."

Brian was stroking Brenda's head and telling her she was safe when she suddenly opened her eyes. She looked frightened and confused until she realized she was in the hospital and Brian was sitting next to her.

Brenda relaxed, but as her medication began to wear off, the realization of what had happened quickly set in and her eyes filled with tears.

"Brian we were wrong!" Brenda cried.

"It wasn't Steve, it was Max who killed all those women. He killed Steve and Julie and Shadow."

"Honey you need to try and relax. It's not good for you to get all worked up."

"Didn't you hear what I said? Max killed Julie and Steve and he was going to kill me!"

"Honey, Julie's not dead, she's still alive."

"She can't be! I saw her! He shot her in the head! She was lying in a pool of blood on the floor!" sobbed Brenda.

"I know honey but I promise you, Julie isn't dead. She's in surgery right now."

Brenda couldn't believe her ears as she anxiously said, "If Julie's not dead, then take me to see her!"

"Honey the doctor said you need to rest and besides, I can't take you to her right now, she's still in surgery."

"Julie's having surgery?"

"That's what I've been trying to tell you."

"Julie's having surgery to remove the bullet that's lodged in her brain. I'm not sure when we'll be able to see her."

"Why don't you try and rest. You've been through a lot and we can talk about seeing your sister after she comes out of surgery."

"There's something you're not telling me isn't there?!"

Brian took a deep breath "Julie's in critical condition and the doctor said she may be in a coma when she comes out of surgery."

"Have you seen her?"

"Just at the house. I didn't know she was alive until one of the rescue guys told me she was taken to surgery."

Brenda stared at Brian's face and fear raced through her body.

"Promise me you'll take me to her as soon as she comes out of surgery. I don't want her to be alone if she doesn't make it."

"I promise," said Brian.

"I need to tell you what happened," said Brenda.

"Only if you're sure you're up to it. If not, it can wait."

Brenda got choked up and could hardly talk as she began telling Brian about Steve shooting Jason.

"I was convinced Steve was the serial killer until Max showed up and shot Steve," said Brenda.

"Max told me his plan to make it look like Steve was the serial killer."

"He was going to tell you that Steve shot at him and he had to kill Steve in self defense."

"Max forced Julie and me into the house and made Julie take off all her clothes. Then he threatened to shoot her if I didn't bind her hands and feet with tape."

Brenda was shaking now and Brian told her he thought she should take a break, but she couldn't seem to stop herself.

Brian's heart went out to her when she broke down crying as she told him about watching Jason being shot and how Shadow had lost his life trying to save hers. Brian gathered Brenda into his arms and said, "None of this was your fault honey. I hope you know that. You were put in a bad situation and by some miracle, you managed to get through it unharmed. I'm really proud of you. Not everyone would have been as brave as you were."

"Shadow and Hank were the brave ones," she said. "They deserve the credit for keeping me alive. If it weren't for them, Max would have killed me too."

"Hank? What'd he have to do with this?"

Brenda told Brian about hiding in Hank's stall. How Hank had charged Max and kept him pinned against the wall while she escaped to the house.

"Hank injured Max's right arm, so he had to use his

left hand to hold his gun. I think that's why he missed me when he pulled the trigger."

Brian was amazed. He thought about all the times he had come close to getting rid of that crazy horse and now he was thankful that he hadn't.

A moment passed before Brenda asked if she had killed Max.

Brian looked at Brenda's tear stained face and shook his head yes.

"He died on the way to the hospital."

Brian took Brenda's hand in his as the door opened and her doctor walked in.

"How are you feeling Brenda?" he asked.

"Tired and a little nauseous."

"Is my baby ok?"

"You don't remember having an ultrasound when you came in?"

"No."

"Well, I'm not surprised. You were in shock when they brought you in, so you were given some medication to help you relax. Your baby is doing fine, but you're going to have to take it easy for a while."

After his examination, Brenda's doctor said, "Everything looks good! I don't see any reason why you shouldn't be able to go home tomorrow."

"I'd like to go up and see my sister if that's ok."

"That's fine with me, as long as you don't get too

tired, but you'll need to check with her doctors first."

"I'll get your discharge papers ready for tomorrow."

"What time can she leave?" asked Brian.

"After my morning rounds, I should think. I'd like to see her before she leaves."

"Well take care of yourself Brenda and I'll see you in the morning."

"Thanks Dr. Reynolds."

A few hours later a nurse came in and Brian asked, if it would be alright if he took Brenda up to see her sister.

"I don't see why not. The doctor gave his permission as long as she's in a wheelchair."

"I'm fine. Why do I have to have a wheelchair?"

"Sorry, I'm just following your doctor's orders," said the nurse.

Brenda tried to be strong, but she lost it when she finally got to see her sister. She started to cry and Brian put his arm around her to try and comfort her. Brenda suddenly had flashbacks of when Allen was in a coma fighting for his life, only this time it was different, because this was her sister.

Julie had undergone brain surgery and the doctor said there was no way of knowing yet, the full extent of the damage to her brain, or if she'd even make it."

"You have to fight Julie," Brenda told her sister.
"You hear me! Don't you dare give up now! My baby and I are going to need you."

Brenda sat by her sister's side until Brian finally said, "You look tired. Why don't we go so you can rest and I'll bring you back up tomorrow before you leave?"
Brenda finally agreed and Brian took Brenda back to her room.

"Where are we going?" Brenda asked Brian, as they drove through town, after her release from the hospital.
"I made arrangements for us to stay in town for a while, so we're going to the Woodland Lodge."
"Why?"
"Because I hired a cleaning crew to come out and clean the house."
Brian looked at Brenda's face and he could see the tears and sadness in her eyes as she turned her head and looked out the window. He knew how hard it was going to be for her to return to the house, so he reached over and took her hand in an effort to reassure her that everything was going to be ok.
Once Brian had Brenda settled in their room he said, "I'm going to go to the house and pick up some

of our things and check on the animals. Is there anything in particular that you'd like me to bring back for you?"

"Just something to wear to bed, my purse and a couple of changes of clothes. Oh, and my toiletries."

"Is that it?"

"I think so."

"Brian, is Hank alright? He was running loose the last time I saw him," said Brenda.

"He's fine. Ornery as ever, but fine. He was in his stall waiting to be fed when I got home."

"When you get to the house, I have a peppermint candy in the bottom of my purse. Will you give it to him and tell him I said thanks for saving my life?"

"Sure, if he'll let me get close enough to give it to him."

Brian reached for the door and Brenda said, "Brian?"

"Yeah honey."

"Would you bury Shadow under his favorite tree in the front yard for me? He loved laying out there where he could keep an eye on everything."

Brian could see the sadness and tears in Brenda's eyes as she talked about burying Shadow.

"Sure honey. Try and get some rest while I'm gone. I won't be long," said Brian, as he gave Brenda a hug and kissed her goodbye.

The next few days were hell for Brian as he tried to

shield Brenda and her parents from the press.
All of the television stations were broadcasting the events that had taken place at the ranch and the news stations wanted to get an interview with Brenda.

Brian had to sneak Brenda and her parents in and out of their rooms at the lodge, so they could get to and from the hospital without being mobbed by the press.

Brian had to have a gate put up at the end of the driveway at the ranch, in order to keep the media away. Police were patrolling the road in front of the ranch, to chase off any over enthusiastic reporters from parking along the road and blocking traffic.

After a couple of weeks, things started to settle down and the reporters gradually began to dwindle away as they chased after news that was more current.

When Brian finally felt it was safe for Brenda to return to the ranch. He asked her parents to wait a week before coming to stay with them in order to give Brenda a chance to settle in.

Brian could feel Brenda's anxiety as the gate opened. Her hands were clenched together in her lap and she looked at Brian for reassurance.

"It'll be alright honey, I promise. I'll be right here

with you, for as long as you need me."

Brian parked the car and as Brenda got out, she noticed the barn door was open and she heard Hank whinny.

Brenda gave Brian a little smile and he said, "Sounds like Hank's welcoming you home. Do you want to go down and see him before we go in? I know he'd like to see you."

"Yes, I think I'd like that."

Hank had his head stuck over the stall door and as soon as he saw Brenda his ears perked up and nickered to her.

Brenda paused as Charger stuck his head out to see what was going on, but it wasn't Charger or Hank that Brenda was staring at, it was Star.

Brenda, confused and surprised looked at Brian.

"I don't understand," she said.

"I think this is where Jason would have wanted her to be, so I called Jason's family and asked if I could buy her."

"I thought she'd make a good horse for our little girl, or boy."

"I'm glad she's here," said Brenda, "and I know Jason would be too."

Brenda ran her hands up and down Hanks face and scratched him between the ears as he nudged her with his nose.

"I think he's happy to see you," said Brian.

"I'm happy to see him too."

"Thanks Hank. Thanks for saving me. I don't think you'll ever have to worry about Brian sending you to the glue factory now!"

"I never said anything about sending him to the glue factory!"

"We know better, don't we?" Brenda whispered to Hank.

Brian walked over and slid his arm around Brenda's shoulder. Hank flattened his ears and shook his head.

"Ok, I get the message!" said Brian, taking a step back. "I guess some things will never change."

"I kind of like his attitude," said Brenda.

As they walked up to the house Brenda looked at the tree where Shadow used to lay. She knew that even though he was gone, he'd be keeping a close eye on everything for her. Brenda walked over to the tree and noticed that Brian had kept his promise to her. There was a mound of dirt with a small plague sticking in the ground. Brenda's eyes filled with tears as she read the plague.

Here Lies Shadow
The Bravest Dog We've Ever Known
And lying next to the plague was Shadow's favorite toy.

"I hope that's ok," said Brian.

"It's perfect," Brenda said tearfully

Brian opened the trunk of the car and got their bags. "I have a little surprise waiting for you inside," he said. "I hope you like it."
Brenda looked at Brian with an uneasiness in her heart. Her first thought was that he had gotten her another dog and she knew she wasn't ready for another dog to take Shadow's place.
Brian unlocked the door and held it open. Brenda, feeling anxious, hesitated for a second. Looking at Brian, she took a deep breath and then stepped inside.
"What in the world...!" Brenda was totally surprised and shocked.
"What do you think? Do you like it?"
Brenda was dumbfounded as she looked around her new kitchen.
"It's the one you were admiring at the home show."
Brenda started to cry and Brian suddenly felt nervous.
"You don't like it," he said, sounding disappointed.
"Oh my gosh, it's so beautiful. I don't believe you did this!" said Brenda. "I love it!"
Still completely stunned, she gave Brian a big hug and then walked around her new kitchen in awe.
"Granite counter tops. I've always wanted granite counter tops. And you got me a new stove and

refrigerator too!"

"It's so beautiful… and you even put in hardwood floors." Brenda said, totally amazed at the transformation.

"It doesn't even look like the same kitchen."

Brian let out a sigh of relief because that was exactly what he had been hoping for.

"Come with me, there's more," he said excitedly.

"More?"

Brenda followed Brian into the nursery where he had set up all of the baby's furniture.

"I asked one of the ladies who was here cleaning, to help me arrange it, but I can move it wherever you want."

"No, it looks great just like it is."

"You even hung the curtains?"

"Well I hung the rod. The cleaning lady ironed the curtains and hung them up for me."

Brenda was speechless.

"Welcome home sweetheart," Brian said tenderly as he wrapped his arms around Brenda's waist.

"I didn't know how I was going to feel coming back here, but thanks to you, coming home has been much better than I ever anticipated. Thank you darling. You have no idea how much this means to me."

Brenda kissed Brian, and as they stood in the middle of the nursery, they thought about the baby and happier times.

Brian was in the kitchen fixing dinner for Brenda while she rested. When she got up, she told Brian she better try to get a hold of Mike to let him know what had happened.

"No matter how I feel about him, I think he has a right to know about Julie."

"I agree. I'm sure if he still loves her he'd want to be here with her."

Brenda took a deep breath as she looked at the phone.

"Would you like me to call him for you?"

"No, but thanks. I think I should be the one to call him."

Brenda picked up the phone and rang his number. When Mike answered, Brenda told him that Julie had been shot and was in a coma. He was shocked as Brenda explained what had happened.

"I just want you to know I haven't told Mon or Dad the reason why Julie was here and not with you. I thought I'd leave that up to you."

"I appreciate that and thanks for calling," said Mike.

"Well you know Mike, despite how I feel about you, you're still Julie's husband, so I thought you had a right to know."

When Mike arrived in town he called Brenda for

directions to the hospital.

Mike was shocked and riddled with guilt when he saw his wife lying there with her head bandaged and tubes and needles running into her body. She was pale and fragile looking and Mike choked up as he watched her clinging to life.

"I'm so sorry honey," he whispered. "I'm so sorry for hurting you like that."

Brenda fought back the feelings of anger she had been holding inside her, as she looked at Mike's drawn, tired face.

Over the next few weeks, Mike made every effort to visit Julie at least a couple of times a week. But as time passed, the number of his visits grew fewer and Brenda's anger towards Mike, became harder for her to control, as she wondered if he was spending that time with his girlfriend. When Brenda voiced her irritation with Mike to her mother, her mother defended him.

Oh, if you only knew the truth mother, you might not be so quick to defend Mike, Brenda told herself.

Chapter 11

A month had passed and Julie was still in a coma. Brenda's parents had been staying at the ranch, but now Brenda's father was packing his things to fly back home.

"I wish you didn't have to leave," Brenda told her father, as he hugged her goodbye.

"Me too honey, but I can't afford to take any more time off work right now. If Julie's condition changes, call me and I'll be on the next flight back."

Mr. Hollister gave the women a goodbye kiss and then he and Brian left for the airport.

"Since Brian's going to work after he drops your father off, what do you say we go into town and look for baby clothes?" suggested Brenda's mother.

"I really don't want to buy a lot of baby clothes until after I have the baby. Then I'll know if I need to buy clothes for a boy or a girl."

"I'll buy lunch… Come on honey. I'd really like to try that cute little coffee shop you told me you liked so well and we could just look at the baby clothes? It'll be fun."

"Alright mother, but you have to promise me you won't go buying things for the baby!"

"Well I can't promise I won't buy anything!"

Brenda gave her mother a stern look and her mother said, "Alright! I promise!"

By the end of the second month, Brenda's patience with her mother had worn rather thin. It seemed like she was always bored and wanted to go somewhere besides home, every time they left the hospital and Brenda was getting worn out.
"Brian, please tell me you'll entertain my mother today for me. If I don't get some peace and quiet pretty soon, I swear I'll have to shoot her!"
"What am I going to do with her?"
"I really don't care, as long as I don't have to deal with her! Why don't you take her to the art museum in Montgomery? Then when she's not looking, you can slip out and leave her there."
"That's not very nice!" chuckled Brian.
"Oh Please."
"No."
"Why? We can go back in a week or two and pick her up."
"Ok honey, I'll figure something out, but it won't be that."
"Have I told you lately how much I love and appreciate you?"
"Yeah, Yeah. You're going to owe me big time for this one!"
When Brian and Brenda's mother had left the

house, Brenda filled the bathtub with bubble bath and slid in.

"Oh my gosh. This feels so good," she told herself, as she closed her eyes and laid back.

When Brenda had finished her bath, she lay down on the bed and was about to drift off to sleep when the phone rang.

"Hello?" she said sleepily.

"Is Brenda Nichols there?"

"This is Brenda."

"Brenda, this is St. Joseph's Hospital. Dr. Forester wanted me to call and let you know that your sister Julie has come out of her coma."

"Julie's awake? Oh my gosh. That's wonderful! I'll be right there. Thank you so much for calling!" Brenda jumped up and quickly hurried to get dressed.

On her way out the door, she grabbed her phone and called Brian.

"Brian, you and mom need to come to the hospital right away! The hospital just called and said Julie has come out of her coma."

"That's great honey, we'll be right there."

Brenda jumped into her car and headed for the hospital.

Brenda anxiously rode the elevator up to the Intensive Care Unit. When the doors opened, she rushed down the hall to her sister's room. Stopping briefly to compose herself before she went in, and trying not to expect too much, she walked in.

Julie's eyes were closed when Brenda entered the room and sat down next to her. She whispered her name and gently took her hand. Julie sleepily opened her eyes and looked at her sister who was sitting next to her. Tears filled her eyes and slid down her face.

Brenda's eyes also filled with tears, as she said, "It's about time you woke up. You had me worried there for a minute."

"How are you feeling?"

Julie tried to speak but Brenda couldn't make out what she was trying to say.

"I'm sorry honey, I couldn't understand you. What'd you say?"

Julie could see the anxiety on her sister's face as she tried again to speak to her.

When Brenda still couldn't make out what she was saying, tears began to well up in Julie's eyes.

Brenda, seeing the fear and frustration on her sister's face each time she tried to speak said, "Its ok honey, we'll have plenty of time to talk when you're feeling better."

Brenda was fighting back her own tears now, as she tried to reassure her sister.

It was only a few minutes later before Brenda could

hear her mother's voice as she came down the hallway. She quickly excused herself, telling Julie she'd be right back and then left the room.
Brenda wanted to explain to them that Julie was having difficulty speaking and that it was upsetting her. Brenda then went on to warn her mother about asking Julie any questions, or bringing up what had happened at the ranch.

Julie kept drifting in and out of sleep as her mother rattled on about Brenda's pregnancy and how she needed to start eating more. Brenda did have to give her mother credit though; she never brought up anything about what had happened at the ranch.
Just as Brenda was about to suggest that they leave so Julie could rest, a nurse came in. She asked if they minded stepping out while the girl from the lab drew Julie's blood.
"Not at all," said Brenda. "We were just getting ready to leave anyway."
"We were?" said her mother.
"Yes we were. Julie needs to rest and like you said, I need to eat."
"Alright then. Goodbye darling," said Mrs. Hollister.
"We'll be back this evening to see you."
Julie nodded as a smile crossed her lips. Brenda bent down to kiss her on the forehead when Julie reached across her body and touched Brenda's hand.

Brenda smiled and said, "I love you too sis. I'll see you later."

Julie closed her eyes and drifted off as they quietly left her room.

Julie's doctor had just walked through the door as they were leaving and Brenda said, "Hello Dr. Forester."

"Hello Brenda."

"I take it you've been in to see your sister?"

"Yes, we were just in with her. She was drifting in and out so we decided let her rest."

"Did you know she can't talk? She tries, but her words come out all jumbled up and you can't understand her!" Brenda's mother said, all flustered.

"Your daughter has some paralysis down her right side due to the trauma to her brain. The paralysis is what's causing her speech and motor skills to be impeded. She's going to need a lot of intensive therapy Mrs. Hollister," he explained.

"So you're saying everything on Julie's right side is paralyzed including her tongue," said Brenda.

"I'm afraid so."

"Oh, dear lord!" said Mrs. Hollister.

"She's going to be alright isn't she? She's not going to be an invalid?" Mrs. Hollister asked, all in a panic now.

"It's still too early to tell just how much damage was done. Your daughter's been through a lot Mrs.

Hollister. She's really lucky to be alive."

"But you do think with therapy she'll be able to talk again don't you?"

"We'll know more after her brain has a chance to heal. Just don't expect an overnight cure. She's going to have a long hard road ahead of her."

"Mom, you need to settle down. Can't you just be happy she's not in a coma anymore?"

"Of course I am. I just want her to be normal again. Is that so awful?"

"That's what we all want, but like the doctor said, it's going to take time and there aren't any guarantees."

"We need to call Mike and let him know Julie's conscious," her mother said.

"We can call him when we get home," Brenda told her.

On the drive home, Brenda's mother fretted about how Julie was going to care for herself when she was released from the hospital.

"I know Mike's a good husband and will try, but I just don't know how good of a caregiver he'll be. I think I should plan on staying with them until Julie's back on her feet."

"Mom, don't you think we should take one day at a time? She just came out of a coma for god's sake, and the Doctor's don't even know what to expect yet! Besides you know Julie, she's a fighter. I'm sure she'll do everything she can to get better."

"But what if she doesn't get better?"

"Well if that should happen, which I doubt, and she does end up needing help, I'm sure between the three of us, we'll be able to figure something out."

"Maybe it would be a better if she came and stayed with me and your father. I'm home all day and it would be easier for me to look after her then it would be for Mike."

"Mom... Stop! Didn't you hear anything I said? We need to wait and see how Julie does with her therapy before we start making any plans. She may be fine and then all your worrying and planning will be for nothing!"

"You're right honey. She's going to be just fine."

As soon as they got out of the car and into the house, Brenda's mother said, "I'm going to call Mike."

"Alright," said Brenda, "but don't go blowing everything out of per portion. Remember, we don't know what's going to happen yet."

But the next thing Brenda knew, her mother was saying, "Mike? It's Julie's mom dear. Julie's come out of her coma, but she's paralyzed down her whole right side and she can't talk!" Mrs. Hollister sobbed. "I know it's just terrible!"

"You need to come as soon as possible."

Brian looked at Brenda and he could see the frustration on her face as she listened to her mother. "Ok, I'll see you tomorrow and we can decide then how we're going to care for her when she's released."

Brian could tell Brenda was ready to strangle her mother. "It'll be alright," he told her. "You and Julie will just have to sit her down and talk to her when she's not so upset."

"Right," said Brenda. "If I don't kill her first."

After a month of therapy, Julie started to get some of her speech back. She was slowly learning to walk again with a walker and her doctor's were very encouraged by her progress. They tried their best to reassure her mother that Julie's prognosis was looking better each day, but she continued to talk about having her come and stay with her and her husband as soon as she was released.

Mike had been coming regularly to see Julie, but Brenda could tell that things were still really strained between them.

As the weeks passed, Mike's visits became further and further apart. Brenda's mother couldn't understand why Mike seemed so distant, or why, now that Julie was doing better, he was coming less and less.

When Julie finally told her parents what had

happened between her and Mike, she thought her mother was going to have a stroke. She had always thought Mike walked on water and could do no wrong, so she was shocked when she heard he had been cheating on her daughter. Brenda felt the reason Mike wasn't showing up, was because he was too embarrassed to show his face after finding out Julie had told her parents about his affair.

Julie had made it clear to Brenda that she would rather stay in the hospital's rehab, then go home with her mother. So Brenda assured her that that was something she needn't worry about. "If it comes to that," Brenda told her, "you'll be more than welcome to come and stay with Brian and I for as long as you want."

"You're get..et..ing a bel..ly," Julie told Brenda, when she came walking into her room.
"Thanks sis. Like I don't already know that!" said Brenda rubbing her swollen belly.
"I ju...st nev..re no..tist it be...fore."
"Well thanks for pointing it out."
"The doctor told me you can go home as long as you have someone around to help you."
"I...know."
"Do you think you feel up to leaving?"
Julie shook her head. "Ye...sss."

"Good, because Brian and mom will be here soon to help me spring you from this joint."

"How..much..long.."

"How much longer is mom staying?"

Julie shook her head.

"I don't know. But once we get you back to the ranch, I'm hoping between you and I and dad, we can convince her that it's time for her to go back home."

Julie started to say something when Brenda said, "Shush, here they come."

Julie had been back at the ranch for two months and her mother was still refusing to leave, despite all of Brenda's attempts to convince her that Julie would be just fine there.

Brenda decided to make one last ditch effort to send her mother on her way.

"Mom, you've been away from home for month's now. Don't you miss being in your own house? I can handle things here and Dad needs you at home."

"Are you saying you and Brian don't want me here anymore?"

"No, of course not. It's just that, Julie's getting better every day and I really think you should start thinking about going back home to dad."

"I suppose he could use my help. I just worry about you two. You've been tired a lot lately and Julie's still not completely back to normal. You may not realize it now, but you're going to need my help when the baby comes!"

"Brian can help me with the baby and if I do need your help, all I have to do is call you. I'll tell you what. Dr. Reynolds wants me to come in for an ultra sound. If I set up an appointment with him so you can see for yourself that the baby and I are fine, will you go back home to dad?"

"I guess so. But only if he says everything's fine."

"Great! I'll call him right now."

Brenda looked at Julie with a wide-eyed glance and Julie had to turn her back to keep from laughing. Thinking her sister was a genius, Julie quickly took the doctor's phone number from the refrigerator and handed it to Brenda.

When Brenda hung up the phone she said, "Ok, it's all set. They can get me in day after tomorrow."

"That's wonderful honey."

"Isn't this exciting Julie? I'm going to be able to see my little grandbaby for the first time," their mother said, as she reached over and rubbed Brenda's stomach.

"That's right mom. Now why don't you call dad and tell him you're coming home this weekend?"

"Not until I know you and the baby are fine! That was the deal!"

"Oh, good lord mom! I can assure you we're both

just fine! You're such a worry wart!" said Brenda, as Julie burst out laughing.

The big day had finally come and Brenda was being followed into the doctor's office by an entourage consisting of her mother, her husband and her sister.

"I hope we can fit all in the room," Brenda whispered to Brian.

He smiled patiently at her and said, "I'm sure it'll be fine."

"I always pictured it being just you and me seeing our baby for the first time."

"Well I can send them away, but then that would mean we'd never get rid of your mother," whispered Brian.

"Good point!"

Brenda was taken into the room first so she could change. Shortly after that her family came in, with her mother leading the way.

"I'm so excited!" her mother told Brian and Julie as they entered the room.

Julie looked at Brian and he smiled and shook his head in despair, as they followed Mrs. Hollister into the ultra sound room.

"The ultra sound tech will be right with you," a young assistant told them, as she was leaving.

"It's so wonderful that they can do this now."

" We didn't have this sort of thing when I was pregnant for you girls."

"We know mom," said Brenda.

The door opened and a middle-aged woman made her way into the crowded room. She smiled as she looked at all the anxious faces staring at her.

"Well it looks like everyone's here."

"Brenda Nichols?"

"That would be me."

"Well my name's Mary and I'll be doing your ultra sound."

"I'm the grandmother and this is Brenda's sister Julie. And this handsome guy is Brenda's husband Brian, the proud father to be."

Brenda let out a sigh and rolled her eyes as she looked at Brian.

Brian had a smirk on his face and quickly turned his head so his mother-in-law couldn't see his face.

Julie also smirked at her sister's obvious dismay and when she noticed the look on Brian's face, she had to turn her head to keep from laughing out loud.

"Ok, let get started," said the tech.

Moments later the tech pointed to the screen and said, "There's the baby's head right there."

Brenda squinted as she looked at the tiny figure on the monitor.

"And if you look right here…. you can see the baby's heart beating."

Julie started to tear up as she looked at her sister. She was happy for her, but she couldn't help but feel a little envious. She had been trying to have a baby for some time, but it just wasn't meant to be. She looked over at Brian who was glowing with pride. It was quite the beautiful moment, until she heard her mother say, "Oh look, it's a little boy! Look right there, you can see his..."

"MOTHER!" yelled Julie.

The tech looked startled as she looked at Brenda and then at the rest of the group with surprise.

"Mom, you knew Brenda didn't want to know the sex of the baby," scolded Julie.

"I forgot! I'm sorry honey, but surely you could see it's a little boy."

When Brenda's mother noticed the displeasure on Julie and Brenda's face, she quickly said, "Maybe I'm wrong!"

Brenda looked at the tech, "Is it a boy?" she asked.

"Your mom's right. It's definitely a little boy."

Brian put his head down on Brenda's shoulder as tears filled his eyes. He had never felt as much emotion or love before, for any two people, as he did right then for Brenda and his son.

Brenda touched Brian's head and said, "You're going to make a wonderful father to our son."

Everyone had tears of joy in their eyes as they watched this tiny little baby, sucking away on his tiny little fist.

Weeks turned into months and as the time slowly passed, other than some short-term memory loss, Julie had made great strides toward a complete recovery.

Despite Mike's efforts to reconcile with Julie, she was never able to get over the fact that he had cheated on her, and eventually she filed for a divorce. A small law firm in Montgomery offered her a job which she accepted, and once she was on her feet she moved into her own place, not far from the ranch.

Brenda, along with everyone else, was growing more anxious with each passing week for Brenda's baby to arrive. No one however, was any more anxious than Brenda's mother, who was calling two and three times a day.

March had finally arrived and it was the first day of spring. The sun was shining and even though it was cold outside, it was still a beautiful day. Brenda had gotten up earlier than usual and was standing at the kitchen window looking out, when Brian walked up behind her and slid his arms around her belly.

"You're up early. Is our son giving you trouble already this morning?"

"No, he hasn't started practicing his karate kicks yet this morning."

"I woke up with a backache and decided I might as well get up and put the coffee on."

"Well then why don't you sit down and let me fix breakfast for you this morning?"

Brian noticed Brenda rubbing her lower back as she poured her coffee and sat down at the table.

"Is your back still bothering you?"

"Not as much now. It seems to be going away."

"I'm going to fix some eggs. Do you want some?"

"I don't think so. I will take some toast though."

Brenda started to get up and Brian said, "I'll get it, just sit down and take a load off."

"Very funny! I wish you were carrying this baby!"

After Brian had eaten, he stacked the dishes in the sink and went out to the barn. Brenda got up to put another slice of toast in the toaster and as she stood there waiting for it to pop up, she felt a strong cramping pain in her stomach. She sat down and held her stomach until the pain subsided.

When Brian returned he found Brenda pouring a cup of coffee and setting a plate of toast on the table.

"You must really be hungry this morning. Are you sure you don't want me to fix you an egg?"

"No, this is fine," said Brenda, holding the cup of coffee out for him to take.

"Just let me wash up and then I'll join you," he told her, taking a sip from the cup and setting it down on the table.

Brian went into the bathroom and as Brenda sat down she felt another cramping pain.

"Brian?"

"I'll be right out."

Brenda sat there holding her breath as pain gripped her stomach. When the pain had finally subsided, she called out to Brian again.

Brian came into the kitchen and found Brenda sitting at the table, holding her stomach and looking at him as if something were wrong.

Worried, he quickly asked, "What's wrong honey?"

"I think you better call the doctor and have him meet us at the hospital."

Brian grabbed the phone, "Is everything ok?" he asked nervously?

"I think my labor's starting."

As Brian was talking to the doctor, Brenda could not recall ever hearing her husband talk so fast, or act so nervous before in his life.

"He said he'd meet us there. What do we now?" he asked Brenda nervously.

"Well I'm going to go get dressed and you need to settle down before you make me nervous!"

"Why don't you take the bag I packed, out to the car."

"Are you sure you have time to get dressed?"

"I'm sure. It's not like the baby's going to be born right this minute, and even if he was, aren't you cops trained to deliver babies?" teased Brenda.

"No we're not trained to deliver babies!"

Brenda noticed Brian franticly searching for her bag, which was sitting in plain sight next to her nightstand.

"My bags over there," she said calmly.

Brian picked up the bag and hesitated. Afraid to let Brenda out of his sight, he said, "Are you sure you're going to be ok in here by yourself?"

"Go! I'm fine! By the time you get back I'll be ready to go."

Brian rushed out of the house and was back within minutes.

"Ready?" he asked nervously.

"Almost," said Brenda. "Can you help me with my shoes? I'm having a little trouble reaching my feet."

Brian's hands were shaking as he slipped Brenda's shoes onto her feet.

"Can we go now?" he asked, getting more anxious by the minute.

"Let's see. Do I have everything?"

Brenda looked around the room and then said, "Can you grab my purse for me?"

"Got it," said Brian. "Now can we go?"

"I guess so," she said, looking around again to make sure she hadn't forgotten anything.

Brian raced for the hospital with his siren blasting,

and his lights flashing. Brenda was starting to get nervous. She hadn't had any more pains since they had left the house and she was afraid that when they got to the hospital, they would tell her it was just a false alarm and send her back home.

Brian pulled into the emergency parking lot and rushed to the passenger side of the car to help Brenda out. He was so nervous he forgot to turn off the flashing lights on his car.

"Brian?" said Brenda. "Don't you think you've drawn enough attention to us?"

"What do you mean?"

"I mean you forgot to turn your lights off."

"Sorry honey. I'm just a little nervous."

When they got inside, Brian rushed over to the desk and told the nurse his wife was having a baby.

"Really? I wouldn't have guessed that," she said, as she smiled and winked at Brenda.

Within a few minutes the elevator opened and an orderly stepped out pushing a wheelchair. He took Brenda upstairs, while much to Brian's dismay, he was told he had to stay and fill out paperwork before he could go up.

Brenda was taken to a delivery room where she nervously waited for a nurse to come in and examine her.

"So are you all ready to have this baby?" the nurse asked.

"You tell me? I had a few pains when I was at home, but I haven't had any since."

"Alright, well let me check and see what's going on down there."

Brenda waited nervously as the nurse checked her.

"Are you going to send me home?"

"Not today," the nurse said with a smile.

"I'm in labor?"

"You've got a ways to go, but I'd say you'll be a mommy before the days over."

"Really? I expected labor to be a lot worse than this!"

The nurse just smiled and then she said, "I'll be back to check on you shortly. If you need me, just push this button here and I'll be right in."

"Thanks."

"Oh, will someone let my husband know where I am?"

"Sure. Now just relax and don't worry about anything. Your doctor's already here and he'll be in shortly to see you."

A few moments later Brian walked into the room looking pale and anxious. He walked over to Brenda and gave her a kiss.

"How are you feeling? Are you in pain?"

"Actually I feel fine, other than this backache."

"I really thought it would be a lot worse than it is."

"Don't look so worried. I'm fine, really."

"I can't believe this is finally happening. It seems like you just told to me you were pregnant."

"Maybe it seems that way to you, but I was beginning to think I was never going to have this baby!"

"Do you want me to call your mother and Julie?"

"Julie, yes. Mother...? Maybe we should wait and call her after the baby's born."

Brian got out his cell phone and Brenda heard him say, "Hey Julie, Brenda and I are at the hospital."

"You mean it's time? She's having the baby?"

"Yeah, she's in labor."

Brian looked at Brenda and said, "You are, aren't you?"

Brenda laughed, "That's what they tell me," she said loud enough for Julie to hear.

Julie laughed. "Ok I'm on my way."

"Ok, we'll see you soon." And then he hung up.

"She said she's on her way."

"I know, I heard her."

"I should of had you tell her there's no hurry. I got the impression from what the nurse said, it'll probably be a while."

The doctor came in and after he had finished examining Brenda, he said, "Everything looks good."

"How are you doing? I know you said you wanted to have a natural birth, but if you need something for pain, I can get you something."

"No, I'm doing fine, but thanks."

"I really haven't had any pains since I've been here. I just have this awful backache."

"How long do you think it'll be before the baby comes?" asked Brian.

"It shouldn't be too long."

"But shouldn't I be having regular labor pains?" asked Brenda.

"Some women do and some don't. Some women come in and with one push the baby's out," the doctor said with a smile . "I'll be back in a little while to check on you."

Brenda and Brian looked puzzled as they stared at one another.

The nurse came in and said, "Your sister's here and wants to know if she can come in?"

"Sure," said Brenda.

Julie popped through the door smiling from ear to ear.

"Hurry up and have that baby! What's the hold up?" she said cheerfully.

"I think I liked her better when she couldn't talk," Brenda told Brian.

Brenda suddenly had a hard, gripping pain. She grabbed the railings on the bed and began to push.

The smile quickly left Julie's face as she and Brian rushed to her side.

"I guess the baby was waiting for you to get here!" said Brenda breathlessly.

"Oh shit! This really hurts!"

"I think the baby's coming!" Brenda yelled.

Brian was ready to run out the door to find the doctor when Julie pushed the panic button.

Within seconds the nurse came rushing in.

"She thinks the baby's coming," Brian yelled in a panic.

"Oh god, I'm never having sex again!" cried Brenda.

"Breathe honey, breathe," Brian was telling her.

"You breathe! I want this baby out!" yelled Brenda as she continued to push.

"Damn it all Brian, this really hurts!"

"Breathe Brenda," said the nurse. "That's right, big breaths."

"Pant like a dog," said Julie. "I heard that helps."

Brenda shot Julie a dirty look and then grabbed her hand and squeezed.

"Ouch, not so hard sis," said Julie.

"Pant like a dog, I heard that helps," Brenda said sarcastically.

"You're doing really well, it won't be long now," said the nurse, trying not to laugh at the two girls.

Finally the gripping pain subsided and Brenda laid back and relaxed.

"There. Is the pain gone?" asked the nurse.

Brenda shook her head.

The nurse looked at Brian and said, "Keep track of the minutes between each of her pains and start timing how long they last."

The nurse started for the door and Brian panicked.

"You're not just going to leave us here alone with her are you?"

"Don't worry I'll be right outside if you need me."

Brenda looked at Brian's white face and told him he better sit down before he passed out.

"You're making me nervous," she told him.

"I'm making you nervous!"

Julie stood there smiling at the two of them, as they bantered back and forth.

Moments later, Brenda cried out again, as another labor pain began.

"Where the hell's the nurse and the doctor?" yelled Brian!

Julie pushed the panic button again, just as the nurse and doctor were coming through the door.

"She's having another pain," said Brian, who was beside himself with worry.

"Let's take a look," the doctor said calmly.

Four hours later the doctor was saying, "You're doing good Brenda."

"Just one more big push."

Brenda pushed as hard as she could and then she heard her baby's first cry.

"It's a boy," said the doctor, "and by the looks of those broad shoulders, he'll probably grow up to be a football player."

"Do you want to cut the umbilical cord?" he asked Brian.

"No! You go right ahead doc," said Brian, who was feeling like he might pass out.

The nurse chuckled as the doctor handed her the baby.

Brian and Julie watched as the nurse suctioned the baby's nose and mouth and then wrapped him up in a blue blanket. She carried him over to Brenda and laid him on her stomach.

"He weighs seven pounds five ounces," the nurse told her. "And he's a perfect little boy."

Brenda looked at her tiny baby's face and hands and her heart felt as if it was going to burst. He looked waxy and his little face was wrinkled, but to her, he was the most beautiful baby she had ever seen.

"Hi there little man. I'm your mommy."

Brenda looked at Brian who had tears in his eyes as he looked at his son.

Kissing the baby's head, she whispered "That's your daddy over there. He's not usually such a softy because he's a cop. He's just happy to see you."

Then she smiled and looked at Brian. "Would you like to hold your son?"

Brian couldn't speak as he picked his son up for the first time and looked into his tiny little face.

"You did good babe," he told Brenda.

"Thanks honey. I try."

"I think he looks like his daddy. Don't you Julie?"

Julie was peering over Brian's shoulder all smiles.

"I don't know. I think he kind of looks like me."

"That's your Aunt Julie. She's been dying to get her hands on you, so be nice to her," said Brian, as he handed the baby to Julie.

"Hey there big guy. My, aren't you the handsome one."

Brenda looked at Brian and smiled, "He's not going to be spoiled!"

"Don't listen to your mother," said Julie.

"Have you decided on a name for my nephew yet?"

Brenda looked at Brian. "I was thinking we could name him Jason Austin Nichols."

Brian thought for a moment and said, "I kind of like that name."

Julie looked at Brenda.

"I understand where you got the name Jason, but how'd you come up with the name Austin?"

"That was Brian's father's name."

"Well Jason Austin Nichols, you and I are going to have a lot of fun driving your mommy crazy when you get a little bigger."

The baby yawned and stretched his arms as Julie smiled and kissed his tiny face.

"Oh my goodness Jason, just wait until grandma sees you!" said Julie.

"She'll never want to leave your Mommy and Daddy's house."

"Oh dear lord. Can't we wait until he's at least twenty before we call and tell her?" asked Brenda.

Julie and Brian both burst out laughing at the look of hopeless despair on Brenda's face as she thought about telling her mother she was a grandma.

The End

Made in the USA
Charleston, SC
20 October 2014